D0838913

Death Therapy

The Destroyer #6

Warren Murphy
and Richard Sapir

AN [e-*reads*]BOOK

New York, NY

Copyright ©1972 by Richard Sapir and Warren Murphy
First e-reads publication 2002
www.e-reads.com
ISBN 0-7592-5323-4

"Before the mountains were brought forth,
Or ever Thou hadst formed the earth and the world,
Even from everlasting to everlasting,
Thou art God. . . ."
Psalm 90

Other books by Warren Murphy and
Richard Sapir also available in e-reads editions

CREATED, THE DESTROYER
DEATH CHECK
CHINESE PUZZLE
MAFIA FIX
DR QUAKE

Table of Contents

Chapter One   1
Chapter Two   11
Chapter Three   20
Chapter Four   27
Chapter Five   33
Chapter Six   37
Chapter Seven   41
Chapter Eight   43
Chapter Nine   47
Chapter Ten   53
Chapter Eleven   57
Chapter Twelve   65
Chapter Thirteen   71
Chapter Fourteen   77
Chapter Fifteen   78
Chapter Sixteen   86
Chapter Seventeen   89
Chapter Eighteen   96
Chapter Nineteen   104
Chapter Twenty   111
Chapter Twenty-One   115

Chapter Twenty-Two   119
Chapter Twenty-Three   127
Chapter Twenty-Four   133
Chapter Twenty-Five   140

Special New
Authors' Introduction

Re-reading an old book (this one was written thirteen years ago) isn't always a happy experience. You have to be awfully dumb to write sixty books in a series and not get better at your craft. So now, when we look at *Death Therapy*, the sixth of *The Destroyer* series, we see a lot of mistakes that we hope we won't make again.

For instance, we got ourselves involved in a lot of nonsense about Remo having plastic surgery after each mission to change his appearance. If we had kept up that particular lunacy, now, a dozen years later, poor Remo would look like an extra in *Night of the Living Dead*. We canned that idea someplace along the way.

There were a couple of gratuitous killings thrown into this book, too. When you're writing about assassins, you can be pretty sure that sooner or later they're going to have to kill people. But at least the targets ought to deserve "termination with extreme prejudice." In writing *Death Therapy*, we hadn't figured that out yet, so our apologies.

The rest of the book stands up pretty well. The story isn't bad either, although some of you might be familiar with it since it was ripped off in a television series, without cash or credit, a few years ago. (That's something we've grown accustomed to.)

Remo and Chiun are just fine, and for the first time Chiun tells his racist little story about how God created mankind. Remo doesn't really believe it and, in truth, we never did either.

— Dick Sapir and Warren Murphy
November 1984

VICTIM'S NOTE

What racist story? Since when is the simple truth racism? Caution, readers. Pay no attention to anything that is in this book. These two moronic scribblers have gotten everything wrong again. It is what they do best.

— Chiun, Master of Sinanju

REMO'S NOTE

Who cares?

— Remo Williams

One

The shot heard around the world had been stilled for almost two centuries when an Iowa banker did something far more significant for American independence than fire a single musket ball at the Redcoats.

He mailed a manila envelope from Lucerne, Switzerland, to his office in the Treasury Building in Washington, D.C.

It was not an unusually large envelope, nor were its contents voluminous. There were ten typewritten pages produced in a rush that morning in his Lucerne hotel suite. Many of the words were incorrectly spelled in a haste of typing fury. He had not used a typewriter since his days at Harvard Business School nearly forty years before.

What the ten pages said was that America still had a chance to retain its independence, but that chance was not very good at all. He estimated his country's prospects of survival at only slightly better than his own, which, in his opinion, were nil.

The ten pages were a memorandum to the president of the United States, but the banker did not dare mail the envelope directly to him. Nor did the banker, who was also an undersecretary of the treasury, dare mail the envelope to his official superior, the secretary of the treasury.

No. If what Clovis Porter, undersecretary of the treasury for foreign affairs, had discovered was true — and he knew as sure as Iowa mud that it *was* true — then his memorandum would never reach the president if mailed directly to the president's office.

For access to the president of the United States was part of the horrifying package for which the international bidding would soon get underway. And Clovis Porter had been just the person to track it down.

1

It could have been hidden from practically any intelligence agent in the world, even if that agent knew what he was looking for. Which he undoubtedly would not have. But the secret could not have been hidden from a banker. And because Clovis Porter was a banker and because he had discovered what was so terrifyingly obvious to him, he was going to die. And there was no one from his own country he could trust to protect him.

Clovis Porter waited, trying not to look too impatient, as the postal clerk pounded the envelope with an inkpad stamp. The clerk asked in French if the gentleman wished to send the envelope registered mail.

No, answered Clovis Porter.

Did the gentleman wish the envelope sent first class?

Not especially, came the casual answer from Clovis Porter.

Air mail?

Uh, yes, why not? answered Clovis Porter absently as he casually glanced around the small post office. He was not being followed. Good. He would not be this safe in Washington. But Lucerne? A better chance indeed.

And how is the gentleman enjoying Switzerland?

"A lovely country," answered Clovis Porter, shoveling some franc notes across the counter at the clerk.

"I think I'll stay another two . . . maybe three . . . weeks."

Clovis Porter told this to the manager of the hotel also. He mentioned his vacation to the Swiss bankers with whom he had had lunch. He mentioned it in the car rental office where he hired a Mercedes-Benz for two weeks.

Then, in his hotel room, he placed a call to his wife in Dubuque, and while waiting for it to be completed, printed in his own hand a message to a bright young man he had met three months before in an office in Langley, Virginia.

The message read:

Mr. A. C. Johnson,
175 Cormider Road,
Langley, Va.
Dear Mr. Johnson. Stop. Large money movements apparent result of market fluctuations. Stop. Nothing unusual. Stop. Just normal.

Stop. Am vacationing for two weeks. Stop. Sorry I could find nothing unusual. Stop. Wasted three months. Stop.

C. Porter.

Then Clovis Porter took off his gray suit, white shirt, and dark tie and folded them neatly into one of the three valises he traveled with. He was middle-aged, yet of such stature that when he dressed in casual touring clothes — slacks and open-necked shirt — it appeared as if he had spent his entire life out of doors.

Perhaps because banking had become something he had forced himself to like, his real love had always been the flat fields of Iowa and the American plains. It would have been nice, he thought, to have spent his last days on the plains with Mildred, perhaps even to have his children and grandchildren by his bedside when his time to depart came.

But that was not to be. He had become a banker, then a Republican fund-raiser, and then an undersecretary of the treasury. And if he had wanted that strongly to live his life with the land, he would not have gone to Harvard Business School in the first place.

Clovis Porter donned his soft Italian-leather walking shoes, and, making sure to take his hotel room key, brought his penciled note downstairs to the manager of the hotel.

He told the manager that the telegram was urgent, read it to the manager with clerks listening, made a small scene about the secrecy and urgency of this message that said all was well. Then, having gathered the focus of attention truly on himself, he stormed away from the manager, not quite accidentally knocking the handwritten message off the counter in the hotel lobby.

Naturally, the manager was forced to retrieve the message from the floor, muttering about "these stupid Americans." Anyone following Clovis Porter could not help but discover what the message said.

He returned to his hotel room and waited for the phone call to get through to Dubuque. In ninety minutes by his wristwatch, it did.

"Hello, hello," came his wife's voice, and hearing that voice, Clovis Porter's strong composure suddenly melted and he gripped the night table, fighting for control of tears he suddenly discovered he still had.

"Hello, darling," he said.

"When are you coming home, Clovis?"

"In about two weeks, Mildred. How are you? How are the children? I miss you."

"I miss you too, dear. Maybe I should meet you in Switzerland?"

"No. Not here."

"Clovis, if I didn't know you better, I would swear you're having an affair with another woman."

"Maybe. You know at this time of life what they say about last flings."

"Clovis, I don't know what's going on, but I can't wait for it to be over."

"It will be soon. I'm just going to relax for a couple of weeks here in Switzerland. How are the kids?"

"They're fine, dear. Jarman is finding himself for the third time this week and Claudia's second child is still expected around late November. We're all fine and we miss you. And we all want you home as soon as possible."

"Yes, yes," said Clovis Porter, and because his knees were becoming very weak, he sat down on the bed. "I love you, dear," he told his wife. "I have always loved you and you have given me a very good life. I want you to know that."

"Clovis? Are you all right? Are you all right?"

"Yes, dear. I love you. Good-bye."

He hung up the telephone and checked out of the hotel. He drove his rented car towards the village of Thun at the base of the Alps. It would be good to breathe the clean mountain air. It would be a good place to die, far from any place where he might endanger his wife and family.

The manila envelope had a chance, just a chance, to reach the president. And then America had a chance, although for the life of him, he did not see how the president, even knowing what was happening, could halt the inevitable flow of events. After all, whom could he trust to stop them?

Still, inevitable events were funny things, and to know what was happening was the first step toward changing their inevitability. His secretary, Miss T. L. Wilkens, would get the envelope within a few days — apparently office instructions. That is what the covering memo said:

4

To: T. L. Wilkens
From: C. Porter
Re: Office Procedure

I wish alterations in the formulation of interoffice memoranda. I think you should change to the pattern we used back at the bank in Iowa. You will see from the attached message that you will take it to the chief executive of the country, showing it to no one but himself under any circumstances. We will use monarch-sized stationery in the future and Number 9 1/4 envelopes.

An agent giving the message a fast nervous perusal might just take it at face value as new office instructions. One had to read the whole note to see that it was more than just a collection of banking instructions. But it contained the message to the president, and if Miss Wilkens held to her guns, refused to leave the note with the president's secretary but waited outside with the stubbornness of the Iowa farmer blood that was in her too, there was a chance. And that was something.

Driving along mountain roads bothered Clovis Porter. The picturesque postcard towns clustered at the foot of mountains bothered Clovis. The winding, tree-shaded roads bothered Clovis.

He wanted to drive on a straight road, straight as a plumbline, and see flat, unending God's country. He wanted to see corn again, the shoots, then the rising stalks making the plains a forest of green. He wanted to see the wheat again, flowing like a golden sea as far as the eye could reach.

He wanted to sit on a man's porch and shake hands on a seed loan, the man's character being his collateral.

But because of his education and his experience in international finance during the Second World War, Clovis Porter was made an undersecretary of the treasury for foreign affairs when it came time to reward Republicans for faithful service.

It had seemed like a career-topping situation. Four, maybe eight, years in Washington, then back to Iowa, knowing you'd done something big, and then spend the last days with friends.

Then there had been Washington, and no amount of hiking or group discussions or even that silly encounter group he had joined when the city just got to him too much . . . none of those things seemed to replace the vitality a man could feel standing on good Iowa earth and talking to friends.

So, when that innocent little phone call came three months before, it did not seem so unattractive to take a world trip, ostensibly to examine international monetary fluctuations for an economic report. That was his cover story.

He knew now that he should have followed his instincts. Turn down the assignment and return to Iowa. But he couldn't; he owed it to the Republican Party and the country to stay.

That was just the logic used on him to send him into the world's money markets looking for the thing that could not be hidden from a man of his sort. And when he found it, he knew he was a dead man and that the best place to die was away from his loved ones, where they could not get hurt.

Dammit, it had started so simply with a phone call from the intelligence people who needed some advice on international currency. Fine. Glad to help. Just a casual questioning. Nothing formal, nothing to bother the secretary of the treasury with. Just a word or two of background.

So on that winter day, he drove from the slush of Washington into the snow-dappled countryside of Langley, Virginia, where he entered a new office building and met a rather pleasant, clean-faced young man named A. C. Johnson, who asked him a very engaging question:

"What does a billion dollars mean to you?"

Clovis Porter had barely finished depositing his coat on a hanger when he began to answer the question.

"In dollars, land, project budgets, or what?"

"In gold."

"It doesn't mean much," said Clovis Porter, sitting down. "Only a handful of countries in the world have that much gold. And those that have it don't use it. They just keep it in a warehouse someplace, and let it maintain the value of their currency."

"Why would a country try to gather up a billion in gold?"

"Just habit," Porter said. The question intrigued him. "In dealing between countries, the dollar is as good as gold. But people have been collecting gold for so long, they've just got the habit. So have countries."

"What could a country buy for one billion in gold?"

"What couldn't you buy?" Clovis Porter said.

"If something were for sale for a billion dollars in gold, could you find out what it was? And who was getting ready to buy it? I mean, could it be kept secret?"

"To anyone who knew what he was looking for, it would stand out like a buzzard in July."

"I take it you would know what you're looking for?"

"Yes sir, I would," Clovis Porter said.

"I'm glad you said that," the young man answered, "because we need a little favor."

And that was it. Clovis Porter, who was tired of Washington anyway, went out into the marketplaces of the world. And he found out which countries were suddenly trying to build stockpiles of gold, and how they were doing it.

And because he was a banker and because he was willing to liquidate all his assets — even $2.4 million took a frenzied three weeks to turn into cash — he found out why they needed the gold.

They were going to bid in an auction. And one billion dollars in gold was the opening bid. And when he found out what was going on the auction block, he knew that America had only a slim chance of survival and that he could not even trust the young Intelligence man who had given him his assignment.

And he also knew that when it was discovered that he had used his personal fortune to learn what was going on, he would be very much a dead man.

So, Clovis Porter mailed the envelope to Miss T. L. Wilkens, then drove out into the Swiss countryside waiting for them to kill him, hoping that they thought his family was unaware of what he knew.

He would be discovered three days later, nude, having attempted, apparently, to swim upstream in the sewer system. Official cause of death: drowning in the excrement of the good people of Thun. There were witnesses, all of whom thought it odd that a man could be walking around the town, incessantly humming a strangely happy song, and then only minutes later take his own life.

The body would be returned to Dubuque for burial, but Miss T. L. Wilkens would not be there to pay last respects to her employer of the last two decades. She would be running for her life, because of a seemingly harmless telephone conversation she had had with Clovis Porter the day before his death.

It was long distance from Switzerland, and before she picked up the call, Miss T. L. Wilkens, a bosomy solid woman with graying hair and bone spectacles, took a freshly sharpened pencil from a tray in front of her.

"Yes, Mr. Porter. Good to hear from you."

"Did you get the manila envelope I mailed?"

"Yes, sir. Came in this morning."

"Good. Good. It was office instructions and I've been thinking that I want to rewrite them. So why don't you just tear it up, throw it away, and I'll prepare a new one when I get back. All right?"

Miss T. L. Wilkens paused and, in a flash, she understood.

"Yes, Mr. Porter. I'm tearing it up right now. Want to hear?"

"Did you read it yet?"

"No, Mr. Porter. Haven't gotten to it yet."

"Well, as I say, just tear it up."

Miss T. L. Wilkens slipped some blank paper from a drawer and tore it neatly down the middle in front of the phone receiver, which nestled under her ample chin.

"Good," Porter said. "See you in a few days, Miss Wilkens. Bye."

And because Miss T. L. Wilkens had indeed read the entire memorandum, she proceeded directly to 1600 Pennsylvania Avenue and would not leave the president's outer office until at 11:00 that night, at her urgent insistence, the president agreed to see the secretary of the undersecretary of the treasury for two minutes. He spoke with her for two hours. Then he said:

"I wish I could offer you the protection of the White House, but as you know, that may not be worth all that much anymore. It's probably the worst place. Do you have any money for travel?"

"I have credit cards."

"I wouldn't use them if I were you. Wait a minute. I haven't carried cash for years. A strange job." The president rose from his seat and went to an outer office. He was back in a few minutes with an envelope.

"There's a few thousand in here. It should last you for a couple of months. And by then you'll know if you can surface again."

"Probably never, sir. It looks pretty bleak."

"Miss Wilkens, we're not out of the box yet. Not by a long shot. We're going to win."

And he ushered the surprised woman to the door and wished her good luck. She was surprised because of his confidence, and in her Iowa farmer's way, she wondered if he were not just acting for her benefit.

But what she could not know was that someone's brilliant, perfect, and thorough plan had a flaw. Precautions had been taken to prevent every existing American agency that could stand in the way of success from even reaching the president's office. But the plan could not take into account an organization that did not exist — and a man who was officially dead.

And now, if the president faced danger from unknown quarters and was unable to trust anyone, let his enemies be blissfully unaware. Because he was still able to unleash upon them the most awesome human force in the nation's arsenal.

The president bounded from his office with new energy and soaring confidence. He went to his bedroom but instead of getting undressed for bed, he took a red telephone from a drawer in his dresser. He dialed a seven-digit number, just as if it were an ordinary telephone.

A thin, lemony voice answered:

"Doctor Smith here."

"It's me," the president said.

"I assumed as much."

"You must see me as soon as possible here. I will leave word that you are to be brought in to me as soon as you arrive."

"I don't think that's wise, sir. We could eventually be compromised and knowledge of us could compromise the government."

"That might not matter very much anymore," the president said. "You must see me immediately. Your group may be the last hope of this government."

"I see."

"I guess you'll be putting that person on alert, Dr. Smith?"

"I'll have to see what we're dealing with first, sir."

"This is the greatest national emergency we have ever faced. You will find that out as soon as you arrive. Now, put that man on alert."

"You are talking to me, sir, as if I work for you. I don't. And in the agreement that established us and the ensuing modifications, you cannot order the use of that person."

"I know you will agree," the president said.

"We'll see in a few hours. I will leave immediately. Is there anything else?"

"No," said the president.

There was a click on the other end of the phone. The man had hung up his receiver. And the president was sure that when that man discovered what had happened to the government of the United States and what was in the process of happening, he would unleash that person.

The president returned the phone to the drawer and then from his pocket took the ten sloppy pages of typing given him by Miss T. L. Wilkens minutes before. He again read the entire contents.

"Well, all right," he said softly to himself. "They asked for it. Now they're going to get him."

Two

His name was Remo.

And when he stepped up to the first tee of the Silver Creek Country Club in Miami Beach, he was mad. Not a raging anger, but a solid, definite annoyance that would not leave.

It was 5:30 A.M., and the reddening dawn sky was just breaking into light as he whacked his drive down the empty fairway and handed the driver to the bushy-haired caddy in the bell-bottoms. The caddy was still rubbing his eyes, apparently not planning to wake up until noon.

He did not speak to the caddy as he marched toward the ball. He did not really even need a caddy, but if golf was his relaxation before his morning exercises, then, by God, he was going to enjoy it like a normal human being.

He had some rights after all, even if normal procedure was violated at will every time Upstairs got a hair up its ass.

He took the next club from the caddy and, barely setting himself, popped the ball toward the hole. Then he exchanged the club for the putter, walked to the green, banged in the ball, and took his driver again.

One would think, what with the awesome resources, the massive computers, the far-ranging network, that Upstairs would once, just once, come into something not as a loosey-goosey, the world's going to end, top maximum priority, be ready by tomorrow, screwball pack of squawking geese.

The man named Remo slammed the drive to the green. When he walked, he seemed to float. His movements were smooth and his golf swing was smooth, the club moving with what he had been told was incredible slowness.

11

He was about six feet tall and average in build. Only the extraordinarily thick wrists set him apart from other men. His face was healing from his last operation and now, with his angular cheekbones and cruel, self-indulgent smile, he looked like an up-and-coming Mafia underboss.

It was the new face after each assignment that got to him. He didn't even have a choice. He would go to a small hospital outside Phoenix, leave with bandages, and then, two weeks later, eyes blackened from the operation, facial muscles sore, he would see what sort of face Upstairs had decided to give him. Or maybe it was just left to the whim of the doctor. It was anyone's choice but his.

The putter was in his hands; feeling the roll of the green, he sent the ball on its way toward the cup. Before he heard the plunk, he was on his way to the next tee.

Whack. Remo drove the ball down the fairway, hooking it from the long dog-leg left. He flipped the driver behind him and heard the caddy catch it.

It was truly the new faces that bothered him. But dead men can't be choosers, can they, Remo, he told himself. He waited by the ball as the caddy puffed his long way from the tee. The caddy's breathless plodding rush toward Remo should have told him something, but he ignored it. The green rose 170 yards ahead. When the caddy reached him, Remo said: "Check out the flag placement, will you?"

The caddy trudged off toward the green. Remo whistled softly to himself. The caddy seemed to take forever.

Why was Upstairs always in a rush? His shoulder hadn't even healed yet from that scrawny mobster in Hudson, New Jersey, who had passed out before Remo's floater punch could land. Remo's hand kept going and so did his shoulder. Now it was just completing its healing. Upstairs must have known that.

The night before, when he had made his evening check from his hotel room, he had dialed the correct number on the scrambler attachment after hearing the first ring, and then he heard something that sounded as if the line were still scrambled.

"Remo. Be at peak by tomorrow afternoon. I'll meet you at 10 P.M., main restaurant, Dulles Airport in Washington. No time for new identity. Come as you are."

"What?" said Remo, checking the scrambler dial again.

"You heard me. Ten P.M. tomorrow night. Dulles Airport." Remo looked at the phone again. It was working.

He stood, clad only in his undershorts, by the bed in his hotel suite. In the next room, he could hear the television blaring. Chiun was still in his third hour of soap operas. The air conditioner hummed almost noiselessly.

"Doctor Smith, I presume," Remo said.

"Yes, of course. Who the hell else would answer this number?"

"I had cause for wonder," said Remo. "For one, I don't peak, not even fast peak, in less than two weeks. And you haven't even put me on alert yet. Two, you yourself arranged the Mickey Mouse switching of identities every time I go to the john. Three, if we're going to run pell-mell into everything, why do we have to bother with the plastic surgery? And four, the next operation I get returns me to something like what I looked like before I got suckered into this lashup. And that's the last one."

"Chiun says you can function below peak and work to it."

"Chiun says."

"Yes."

"What about what I say?"

"We'll talk about it tomorrow night. Good-bye."

Then the click of the phone. Remo gently removed the plastic and aluminum scrambler device, and with his right hand slowly squeezed until the circuits began to pop under the cracking plastic. He kept on squeezing until what he held in his hand was a solid rod of crushed electronics.

Then he went to the next room where the television was on. Sitting two feet from the set, in a lotus position, was a frail wisp of an Oriental in robes, his white beard flowing from his parched face like the last strands of pale cotton candy.

He was watching Dr. Lawrence Walters, psychiatrist at large. Betty Hendon had just revealed to Dr. Walters that her mother was not really her mother but her father posing as an upstairs maid in the house of Jeremy Bladford, the man she loved but could never marry because of her teenage marriage to Wilfred Wyatt Hornsby, the insane recluse billionaire, who was even now threatening to close down Dr. Walters's new clinic for the poor.

"Chiun," yelled Remo. "You tell Smith I could function below peak?"

Chiun did not answer. His bony hands remained crossed in his lap.

"You wanna get me killed, Chiun? Is that what you want to do?"

The room was silent but for Dr. Walters's peroration on why it was important for people to accept themselves as people and not as others expected them to be.

"I'm gonna unplug that set, Chiun."

A slender finger with a delicately tapered nail of almost equal length rose to the old man's lips.

"Shhhh," said Chiun.

Fortunately, the fade-out organ music came on and an obnoxious child jumped on screen, breaking up her mother's card game to tell her about the state of her teeth. The mother seemed pleased. So did the other players, all of whom had four of a kind, and they demanded to know what dentifrice the child used.

"You need not be at peak all the time, any more than a car must drive at ninety miles an hour all the time."

"When a car's in a race, it helps to be able to move fast."

"Depending upon what or whom one is racing," Chiun said. "A car need not run fast to beat a turtle."

"And the whole world's my turtle?"

"The whole world is your turtle," Chiun said.

"But suppose I run into a very fast turtle?" Remo asked.

"Then you pay the final dues of our profession."

"Thanks. It's always a comfort having you around. I'm into an assignment by tomorrow night."

"Work the walls then," Chiun said. "And a word of caution, my son."

"Yeah?"

"Anger will destroy you faster than any turtle. Anger robs the mind of its eyes of reason. And you live by your mind. We are weaker than the buffalo and slower than the horse. Our nails are not so sharp as the lion's. But where we walk, we rule. The difference is our minds. Anger clouds our minds."

"Little Father," interrupted Remo.

"Yes?"

"Blow it out your ears."

Remo turned from the sitting room, back into the bedroom, and began to work the walls, first running toward one, then bounding back, then toward another and bounding back, then off a wall in a corner and onto the adjacent wall, and back and forth, from wall to wall, building speed, until finally he was moving like a blindingly fast tapeworm, around the room, on the walls, his feet not touching the carpeted floor.

It was a good exercise. It was a good way to work off energy and anger, Remo thought. Chiun was right as he had always been right. The difference was the mind. Most men could use only a small percentage of their coordination and strength. At peak, Remo could use almost 50 percent. And Chiun, elderly Chiun, the master of Sinanju, the trainer of Remo and the father Remo never had, could muster more than 75 percent of his capabilities.

It was merely doing all the time what most men were capable of doing only in rare instances.

Remo waited for the caddy to plod his way back. He could not see the flag on the raised green, surrounded by the deep sand traps. The wind was moving left to right and the grass smelled deep and rich and good from the constant care. To the left of the fairway a few twigs cracked, as though crushed by a heavy animal. The noise came from a clump of trees bordered by hedges.

The caddy returned. He was breathing heavily and barely got out the words.

"Eight feet behind the lip of the green, just along the line of the sand trap. The green's fast and the grain is toward you. The green slopes away from you downhill."

The caddy made a slanted motion with his hand indicating the angle of slope.

"It's a hundred and seventy yards. The way you been shooting, you ought to take a pitching wedge."

And then Remo realized he had not been playing his game. In anger, he had just been shooting for score, instead of carefully placing the ball in a sand trap here or in the rough there, and intentionally putting for imaginary holes several feet from the real hole. He had been playing his best possible game and in front of a witness.

"You're something else, Mr. Donaldson," the caddy said using Remo's latest name.

"Give me the four iron."

"The way you been shooting, Mr. Donaldson? I've never seen anybody shoot like you."

"What are you talking about?" Remo asked casually.

"Well, eagle-eagle is a pretty good start."

"You must be hung over," Remo said, taking the four iron. "You're not awake yet. I got a bogey and a par. I know what I shot. What were you smoking last night?"

Remo set his feet very carefully and took two awkward backswings. Then he sliced a sweet curving shot 170 yards — 70 yards forward and 100 yards into the next fairway.

"Damn," said Remo, throwing his club ahead of him in the plush fairway. "And I had a good game going."

The caddy blinked and Remo carefully watched his eyes to see if the caddy would forget those first two holes. The answer would be in his eyes.

But the eyes said nothing, because they were no longer there. A red gash splashed through them to his skull, and Remo had heard the whirring of the bullet before he heard the crack of the shot from the clump of trees bordering the fairway.

The shot spun the boy around, club bag spilling the irons and woods wildly onto the fairway. Remo ducked behind the spinning body, using it as a sandbag. When the boy hit the ground, Remo hit the ground simultaneously, flattening to the contours of the young man. Two more high-power slugs thwapped into the boy's body. No crossfire, Remo thought. He could tell by the heavy impact on the boy that whoever was in the clump of trees was using heavy stuff. Maybe a .357 Magnum. He was also zeroing in.

The boy's body jumped again. Whoever it was, was using a single shot rifle. And because of that he was going to die.

A pause, and the body thumped again. Remo was off. First fast, sideways without changing directions, a bullet behind him. Stop, slow roll to the right, letting the marksman overload. From right to left he moved, traveling the fairway like a pinball, closing the distance between himself and the sniper. And then he realized that there were three. A shot spit up mud at his feet, and then two men emerged from the bushes, one on each side of the rifleman, their faces blackened like commandoes, their uniforms dull green, their boots black and high and polished like paratroopers. They wore black stocking caps, and they came out wrong, moving one behind the other. The first man held a short machine pistol, inaccurate beyond forty yards.

The golf shoes were no help. Real speed was hindered by spikes. Change of direction came not from equipment but from within. The great football players like Gayle Sayers had it, doing things that seemed impossible. And they were impossible to the eyes that believed balance was a matter of footwork. The best sole for movement was the sole of his foot, and the spikes were slowing Remo down, as he angled to set the three men in a line so that only one could shoot at him at a time.

A roll, a fast stop, and another roll got rid of the spiked shoes with the help of short kicks; now Remo was padding the heavy damp grass of the fairway in his stockinged feet. Remo moved head-on into the forty-yard range of the first man, and the middle man brushed the front man slightly in an effort to establish his own line of fire. The front man stopped for a moment.

Remo went into a straight speed line and was on the leader in a flash, his right thumb rigid, making a sweeping arc up as he closed in. By the time he was arms' length from the leader, the thumb was driving and then the thumb bit deep into the first man's groin, sending him careening back with a pathetic lip-surrendering "ooh" into the second man. The "ooh" was very soft, which was not surprising, since his left testicle was now adjacent to his lower lung.

With his left hand, Remo brought his fingernails up to the shin of the second man who was trying to get off a shot with his machine pistol. The fingernails went through his face as if it were head cheese.

And then, unbelievably, the sniper who was reloading, stood up and threw away his rifle. He did not reach for his .45-caliber sidearm, but stood in the karate *sanchin dachi*, feet curved in, pigeon-toed, arms curved slightly in front, fists rigid.

The man was tall and lean and hard, the kind of man whose face gave Texas its reputation. His fists were the size of pound coffee cans. He towered over the hedges. Now he waited calmly for Remo's assault, the glint of his teeth matching in brilliance the colonel's eagles on the shoulders of his uniform.

Remo stopped.

"You gotta be kidding, Mac," he said.

"Step up, little boy," the colonel said. "Your time has come."

Remo chuckled, then put his hands on his hips and laughed out loud. He stepped back, out of the rough. The man with the displaced testicle had passed out. The other, with the split face, was writhing on the ground in a growing bath of blood, his khaki fatigues darkening.

The colonel looked at the two of them, then at Remo, and then began softly to hum to himself.

Remo took another step back and the colonel took a step forward. He moved jerkily to his right as he moved forward, obviously in preparation for an inverted fist, low thrust.

"Who taught you that ding-a-ling move?" Remo said, dancing backwards, but not so far that the man could use a quick draw on his .45.

"C'mon, you traitorous punk," the colonel said. "I'm going to cleanse America of you."

"Not with an *uraken shita-uchi*," Remo said. "Not by you; not by that move."

"Stand still and fight," the colonel said.

"Not until you tell me who taught you that nonsense," Remo said.

"Agreed," the colonel said thinly. "The U.S. Special Forces," and then he moved forward, sending a blindingly fast right hand snapping down towards Remo's face. Unfortunately for the man, his follow-through was a bit more thorough than he had planned. His aim kept on going, out of its shoulder socket, assisted by Remo — who pulled the man forward, then set him tumbling into the air, to land face-first in the sand trap next to the third green.

With a crack of a semi-closed fist, Remo sent the back of the skull deeper down into the sand, where it could not be removed by a simple blast of a sand wedge. He did this while keeping his left arm straight out of courtesy to the country club which would soon be shocked to find that a Special Forces colonel had, in a small way, become a permanent part of the great third hole, dog-leg left.

Then Remo neatly finished off the other two soldiers. Strange, how peaceful men were in death. They always shared graves in harmony.

He moved on to the caddy on the chance, the very slim chance, that the boy might still be alive. He wasn't.

Then Remo walked off the course, leaving by the 17th hole, adjacent to a small side road. The shoulder of his blue-gray golf shirt was torn slightly where it had been nicked by a bullet. And Chiun had assured Smith that Remo could function off peak. That was enough to make Remo angry all over again.

But his anger would fade the next day when he saw Dr. Harold Smith's lemony face dissolve in shock as Remo assured his chief that no, their secret organization, CURE, was no longer secret to someone. And neither was Remo Williams, the man known as the Destroyer. Remo had the nicked golf shirt to prove it.

Three

On July 4th, as America celebrated a long hot weekend and politicians made speeches about the cost of liberty to people waiting for free beer, an American Air Force general named Blake Dorfwill, 48, upped the retail price of that liberty on the world markets by doing something he was trained to do very well. He bombed a city.

St. Louis.

He used a ten-megaton device capable of destroying four St. Louises and contaminating most of Missouri. The damage it actually caused was a very big hole in a garbage dump and minor radiation damage to the garbage.

Air police, military police, and the FBI surrounded the dump and assisted Atomic Energy Commission personnel in removing the untriggered weapon.

Major General Blake Dorfwill caused more damage with his person. He destroyed a home television antenna, the roof of a porch, and a porch swing in a suburb of Springfield. He was removed with sponges and rubber bags. When the owner discovered that the thing that had come crashing into his house was an Air Force general, he demanded double-the-cost damages, including payment for the loss of television reception for a week, causing extreme discomfort and alienation of his family. When he was paid immediately and in cash, he descended into severe depression, haunted by the possibility that he might have demanded and collected five times as much.

The co-pilot of the bomber, Lieutenant Colonel Leif Anderson, explained to the FBI, his commanding officer, his commanding officer's commanding officer, the Central Intelligence Agency, and a Dr. Smith, a thin gaunt-faced man newly appointed to the president's staff, that General Dorfwill had taken the plane out of formation while on a training flight from Andrews Air Force Base near Washington.

According to Colonel Anderson, General Dorfwill ignored his questions and just kept flying on to St. Louis where he released the bomb. Colonel Anderson pointed out that the device required two men to trigger it and he would not do so.

"Were you asked?" asked the gaunt-faced Dr. Smith.

An Air Force general seated at the table looked at the thin civilian as though he had just released gas. But the civilian was undeterred. "Were you asked?" he repeated.

"No, I wasn't," said Lieutenant Colonel Anderson, who then launched into a description of altitude, release time of the weapon, air traffic patterns.

"Did the general explain to you why he was veering off course?" Dr. Smith interrupted.

The Air Force general at the table audibly exhaled his exasperation at the stupidity of a civilian who could conceive of a general explaining anything to a lieutenant colonel.

"No," said Colonel Anderson.

"And during the flight, did he say anything?"

"No," Anderson said. "He was humming."

"What was he humming?"

The men sat around a long boardroom table, under fluorescent lighting in a special Pentagon meeting room. The four-star Air Force general pounded the table with the flat of his hand, hard enough to make the lights flicker.

"Dammit, what difference does it make what he was humming? A nuclear device was released on an American city. We're trying to determine how to stop it from happening again. I don't see, Dr. Smith, how in a pig's ass what the man was humming would matter."

Smith showed no response to the verbal assault.

"Colonel," he said. "What was the man humming?"

Lieutenant Colonel Leif Anderson, a robust, youngish-looking man in his thirties, looked anxiously at the general. The general shrugged his shoulders in disgust. "Answer him," he said in a tired voice.

"Well, I'm not sure," said the colonel.

"Hum a few bars," said Dr. Smith.

At this, the FBI men became annoyed. The lieutenant colonel looked to the general. The general just shook his head in disbelief. The FBI men stared at Smith.

"Hum a few bars," repeated Dr. Smith, as if he were a bandleader trying to satisfy a drunk's request.

"Da da da da dum da dum dum da da da da dum dum," said Anderson in a near monotone, a Rex Harrison cross between singing and talking.

Everyone at the table looked at Dr. Smith. He took a pad from his pocket and began to write. "That's da da da da dum da dum dum da da da da dum dum?" he asked.

"Oh, this is too goddam much," said the general.

"It is somewhat unusual," said one of the FBI men.

"Let's go through that again, if you please," said Dr. Smith.

"You are from the president's office?" said the general.

"Yes," said Smith without looking at the general. "Let's hear that song again."

"I've never seen you at the White House," the general said.

"You haven't checked my credentials?" asked Smith.

"Yes, I have."

"Good. Then, unless you wish to call the president to question his judgment, we will all listen to the song again."

Lieutenant Colonel Anderson flushed red. If his first rendition approached monotone, his second was the definitive version of monotone.

"Da da da da dum da dum dum da da da da dum dum."

"Could you put a bit more life in it?" asked Dr. Smith.

"Oh, Jesus Christ," said the general, dropping his head in his hands. The FBI men began to smirk. The CIA man walked out of the room, announcing he was going to relieve himself.

"More life, please," asked Dr. Smith calmly.

Lt. Col. Anderson nodded and reddened even more. He looked briefly, imploringly, at the ceiling, then hummed again as well as he could. When he was finished, he looked at Smith. "It's like a tune I've heard before," he said apologetically.

"Thank you. Now, you said General Dorfwill took off his parachute?"

Colonel Anderson nodded.

"Did he ever say to you — any time in the past — who had transferred him to Andrews Air Force Base?"

"What difference does that make?" boomed the general. "It so happens I did."

"And how do you spell your name?" asked Dr. Smith calmly.

"General Vance Withers. V as in Victory; A as in Assault; N as in Nation; C as in Constitution; E as Elite. Vance. W as in Win . . ."

"Thank you, general. That will be more than enough. And you can be reached?"

"Here at the Pentagon."

"And you live where?"

"Alexandria, Virginia."

"Good. Can I reach you there by phone at night?"

"Yes. Anything else?"

"No. Not of you," Smith said and turned back to Colonel Anderson, thinking that Remo would appreciate his finding out Withers's address. Remo did not like wasting his time hunting for his targets.

"Did you protest when General Dorfwill took off his parachute, Colonel?"

"He was a general, Doctor . . . Doctor . . ."

"Smith."

"He was a general, Dr. Smith."

Smith made a note on a pad. "Pursuit planes picked you up over Springfield. And they noticed something peculiar when General Dorfwill bailed out, correct? Would you expand on that, Colonel?"

"Peculiar? Well, he went out without his parachute. That's peculiar."

"Something he did on the way down."

"Oh yes, he went down with his hands moving. As if he were in a parachute. As if he were working the riders of the chute. That's what the pursuit pilots said."

"I don't suppose any of you gentlemen have photographs of General Dorfwill's expression as he dropped?" asked Dr. Smith.

"Unhappiness," said General Withers. "Take my word for it. Unhappiness."

The colonel laughed. The FBI men laughed. Finally, the general laughed at his own joke. Dr. Smith didn't laugh. "I don't think so," he said and returned his pad to his pocket. "Thank you all. I have everything I need."

When the peculiar doctor from the president's office left the room in the Pentagon, General Withers shook his head and whistled softly. "And that's what's close to the president," he said.

A murmur of disbelief filled the room. General Withers then began what he considered to be important questioning. Flight positioning. Radio communications. Operational orders. He did so leaning across the table, his jaw thrust forward, his eyes keenly fixed on whomever was speaking. He had a strong and attractive face that had graced several news magazines.

He would have that face for approximately fourteen more hours, until it was mangled into jelly on his own pillow in his own bed in his own home in Alexandria, Virginia. So swift and silent would be his destruction that his wife would wake up only when she felt something wet on her shoulder and turned to tell her husband to stop slavering in bed.

General Withers had committed no crime other than being a possible link in a chain that an organization called CURE wanted broken up at any cost. His signature on the transfer papers of General Dorfwill was his own death warrant.

That signature was verified within forty-five minutes after the peculiar Dr. Smith left the conference room in the Pentagon. Within an hour and a half, photographic blowups were on their way to Smith. Blowups of 16-mm film, obviously shot from a plane, of a man falling. As he looked at the pictures, the photo lab technician thought to himself, funny thing. The man floating toward his death seemed incredibly unconcerned by the whole thing. He leaned over with a magnifying glass to look at the face in one of the pictures. The falling man's lips were pursed, almost as if he were whistling some sort of tune on the way down to the ground. But, of course, that was absurd, the technician told himself.

Within a very few hours, a detailed psychological examination of the photos would be made, and the psychologists' reports and Dr. Smith's interview notes would be coded and fed into a giant computer system at Folcroft Sanitarium in Rye, New York, coded for a matchup with the known facts concerning Clovis Porter.

And the computer would whir around for a while, considering and rejecting possibilities, and then it would tap out: "Need exact details on Clovis Porter death. What did he do in his last moments? Ascertain if he was humming or whistling."

Within minutes, a giant information-gathering apparatus would be at work, and it would end with a European banker doing a favor for a wealthy client. The banker would never know that he had at that instant become a part of a crime-fighting network known as CURE.

If he was lucky, he would never hear of CURE, because that is how CURE was designed. Because CURE was not something for the United States to be proud of. CURE, founded years before when the clouds of chaos and anarchy hung over the American future, was simply an admission that the United States Constitution did not work.

The man who made that admission was the president of the United States. The war against crime was being lost. Crime was growing. Chaos was growing. America would soon go under or become a police state.

A young president made a choice. He could not let the nation's law enforcement armies run wild and so he created an extra-legal force to fight crime. He created CURE. So that no succeeding president could extend his powers through this extra-legal force, the contract stipulated that the president could issue only one order: disband. Everything else was a request.

And so that CURE would not itself become too powerful, it was limited to only one man who could use force. That man had been picked wisely. He had been a normal human being who, CURE had decided, could die without being missed. So in a public electrocution, after a neat, all-ends-tied-tightly frame-up, the young Newark policeman was electrocuted but survived and awoke to become CURE's only weapon: The Destroyer. Remo Williams.

He was the third man to know of CURE. And when his recruiter became compromised in a hospital bed from which he could not escape, the third man, Remo Williams, was ordered to make it two. And two it had been ever since. Remo Williams and Dr. Harold K. Smith, the man who ran CURE, and who sometimes granted the requests of presidents who would ask . . . only ask . . . him for help.

They were the two who knew. But around the nation and the world, thousands worked for CURE without even dreaming of its existence. Federal agents, grain inspectors, customs inspectors in other countries, petty criminals . . . all were part of a worldwide information-gathering service that fed facts into the ravenous CURE computers so they could analyze crime. And now the newest operative was a young European banker who was doing a favor for a wealthy client by trying to find out what someone named Clovis Porter had been doing in the moments before his death.

Four

But it was not Clovis Porter who was being discussed that night in Washington.

Washington watched the Air Force make its official announcement concerning the St. Louis incident. A fuselage tank had fallen from an aircraft into a St. Louis garbage dump. Yes, it was a nuclear bomber. No, no nuclear weapon was dropped on St. Louis. No, such a weapon would not have exploded even if one had dropped. Yes, the pilot fell to his death after the incident. A tragic accident. Yes, it is standing policy that no nuclear weapons are flown over American cities.

Then why, asked the pushy reporter as television lights glared on the marble-calm face of the public information officer, *then why was this bomber flying over St. Louis?*

Navigational misfunction.

Could it happen again?

Not one chance in a million.

When the butler in the large plush living room whose curtains were drawn to Adams Street in Washington, D.C., turned off the television set at the nod from the ambassador, titters were heard through the gathering. Cocktail glasses began to tinkle. One man guffawed.

"It is not that America lies," commented the Urdush ambassador. "It's just that it lies so badly. Perhaps more practice is indicated."

"You people fell into a bit of a muck, didn't you?" asked the British air attache of an American admiral. The admiral answered icily that he was unaware of just what muck the British colonel was referring to.

"Really, old boy, it's common knowledge that you people plopped a nuclear bomb on top of one of your own cities."

"I was unaware of that," said the admiral.

"Well, let's hope your voting public remains so blissfully unaware. Bad business, nuclear warheads, what?"

The French ambassador's wife attempted to diffuse the tension. She asked why military men always appeared so much more sexually alive than other men.

The British colonel accepted the compliment, noting that all men were always more alive when in the presence of beauty.

"Oh, Colonel," laughed the wife of the French ambassador.

"I have noted that military men in the upper ranks, and particularly those who defend countries which are still powerful in the world, have less time for sexual expression," the admiral said.

The smile on the face of the French ambassador's wife became cold without a millimeter's change in smile.

"Well, we all have problems, don't we, Admiral?" said the British colonel unconcernedly.

The French ambassador's wife was wearing an almost see-through blouse, which, on this cocktail circuit, attracted as much attention as a general's star — namely, none.

Then the buzzing of the reception suddenly subsided and the French ambassador's wife saw the blond flowing hair enter the room, then the face, a cool perfection of beauty, and then the smile that made men gasp. It was a smile as dazzling as diamonds and as natural in its awesome beauty as a Norwegian fjord.

The smile of the wife of the French ambassador slowly settled into a thin, muscleless resignation. Other women forced themselves to appear unthreatened, watching closely the faces of their men. They watched mouths open, tongues lick lips, and one unfortunate woman saw her husband sigh. She made immediate and disastrously calculated comment on her husband's age. He responded honestly, "I know, dammit," and it would be weeks before he slept with his wife again.

"By Jove, who is that?" asked the British colonel.

"That is Dr. Lithia Forrester," said the French ambassador's wife. "Stunning, isn't she?"

"She's the most beautiful woman I've ever seen," said the colonel.

"She looks healthy," conceded the American admiral. He was thinking about the firmness of her breasts, which moved with youthful, unfettered grace under the softly draped black silk gown she wore.

"Healthy? Is that all you can say?" commented the British colonel.

The admiral looked into his martini, then back at the colonel's truly shocked face. "In twenty years, she may be built like a balloon. Nothing lasts. Nothing."

"In twenty years, Admiral, she will still be the most beautiful woman I have ever seen. Ever. And I am not talking about Washington or Paducah or the bridge of a ship. I am talking about the world."

"A tit, Colonel, is a tit. A nose is a nose. And a mouth is a mouth. They all become remarkably the same in the grave."

"But we are not in the grave now, sir," the British colonel protested. "At least not all of us."

"Oh, she's coming over here," said the French ambassador's wife.

"Hello, dear," said the French ambassador's wife. The British colonel adjusted his tie and came to a relaxed attention, almost clicking his heels. The admiral took another sip of his martini.

"I'd like to introduce you gentlemen to Dr. Lithia Forrester. Lithia is such a good friend of the embassy," said the ambassador's wife. "Doctor Forrester, Lithia, this is Colonel Sir Dilsy Rumsey-Puck, air attache of the British Embassy. Dr. Forrester. And this is . . . Admiral, excuse me, but I don't believe I know your name."

"Crust. James Benton Crust. You can call me Admiral."

The ambassador's wife flushed at the grossness. The colonel, Sir Dilsy Rumsey-Puck, glowered. And Dr. Lithia Forrester laughed uproariously, reaching to Admiral Crust's arm for support. Admiral Crust could not contain a guffaw, even though he tried.

"Admiral, I am so glad to meet you," said Dr. Lithia Forrester.

"You can call me Jim," said the admiral. "But don't touch."

Lithia Forrester laughed gloriously again and with the entire room secretly watching her — secretly, because men had caught the messages in their women's eyes — she leaned forward and gave Admiral James Benton Crust a kiss on the cheek.

"Is that touching, Jim?" she asked.

"No. That's allowed," he said.

"You know each other then," said the French ambassador's wife.

"No. Just met," said Lithia Forrester.

"Oh," said Colonel Sir Dilsy Rumsey-Puck. And when Lithia Forrester repeatedly turned the conversation to Admiral Crust, the French ambassador's wife excused herself, and finally Colonel Rumsey-Puck lowered the Union Jack and went to join the rest of the party. He had never understood just what it was that had made America so successful in the first place, but whatever it was, the middle-aged admiral obviously had it.

Rumsey-Puck had surrendered after trying to interrupt Dr. Forrester's comment on the tragic General Dorfwill, who had been at her therapy institute and one of those who suffered what she called "the power syndrome." They were easy to cure because they were not really sick, just responding normally to abnormal stimuli.

"It's almost like a football player's knee," Dr. Forrester had said. "The player is healthy. The knee is healthy. But he gets knee injuries because the knee was not designed to take the pressure of 250 pounds running 100 yards in 10 seconds."

"We noticed in Burma," said Colonel Sir Dilsy Rumsey-Puck, "that men who had . . ."

"Excuse me, Colonel," said Dr. Forrester, "but men groping around the jungles are not the same thing as men who hold responsibility for nuclear power. I think our nation has done remarkably well in not blowing up the whole bloody world. I dare say, I would not sleep at night if lesser men controlled that sort of power."

Then she turned back to the admiral who somehow had seemed to grow an inch and a half. Colonel Sir Dilsy Rumsey-Puck bowed slightly and excused himself. And Lithia Forrester went back to explaining how she could have cured poor General Dorfwill if she had simply had time to work with him.

Rumsey-Puck saw her leave the party shortly into the evening, shaking hands with the admiral. When she was out of the main room, the women became more alive.

As Lithia Forrester left the building, she scarcely glanced at her chauffeur but settled down in the back seat of her Rolls-Royce to mull over a very significant problem. She mulled it over through the streets of Washington and into the Maryland countryside. She mulled it over through the gates of the Human Awareness Laboratories Inc., through the long winding roadways, the 6.3 miles of road leading to the ten-story building surprisingly set in the middle of the lush greenery and rolling hills.

She mulled it over on the elevator to the tenth floor, where she stormed into a round and luxurious parlor-type room.

And when she was sure she was alone, she slipped out of her black silk gown and threw it against a wall.

"Balls," she said.

She did not mind losing General Dorfwill. That was part of the plan. He had had to die, since one did not want the poor nit back on the ground, being asked why he had decided to drop a nuclear bomb on St. Louis.

And Clovis Porter had to be killed. One could not possibly have known that he would stumble on the program. Granted, he was a banker, but he was a Republican. And from Iowa. He should have done what was expected of him, investigate and find nothing. When he dug too deep, he had to be killed.

But the Special Forces colonel was a mistake. A grievous costly mistake. And it was not the mistake itself that was so costly, it was the new element it disclosed.

Lithia Forrester strode to a marble-topped desk and withdrew a yellow pad from a drawer. She made a diagram with a string of dots along an arrow. The first dot was the telephone company security man. He had discovered the special scrambler line to that Folcroft Sanitarium. That was the second dot. And the president had used that line the night Porter's secretary had shown up at the White House. Then the conversation about "that special person." And that was the last dot. The "special person" in Miami Beach. Obviously some sort of special investigator. And that was where she had made her mistake.

Since the program was proceeding, that person had to be eliminated. But she was wrong in using the Special Forces colonel. It had seemed right. He could reinforce his weak masculine self-image. The big problem had been to convince him to use other men too, instead of playing Tarzan by himself. Well, she had convinced him.

So why was that agent, that Remo Donaldson, still alive? How had the colonel managed to get himself killed? That was the trouble with Special Forces people, with commandoes and Rangers and People's Special Liberators. If anyone could botch the simple assignments, it was those daredevils. The staff officers were right. You don't trust important missions to those zanies. Dorfwill would have done the assignment well. Even Clovis Porter would not have failed.

One human being named Remo Donaldson, and suddenly people start turning up mangled. Well, Mister Remo Donaldson, you are about to meet people who do not fail.

And on the yellow pad, she made a large X over the last dot. Then she looked up at the darkening sky, for she was standing underneath a giant Plexiglas dome, the latest in designs for living. She knew it was the latest because she had designed it. And she had never yet designed anything that failed.

Five

The man who was the last dot on Lithia Forrester's yellow pad was at that moment at Dulles Airport outside Washington, trying to find a way to explain to his employer, Dr. Harold K. Smith, just why he was quitting.

"This is a very special case," Smith said. "Perhaps the most important we have ever faced."

Remo Williams, known to Lithia Forrester as Remo Donaldson, decided on the direct approach.

"Blow it out your ears," he said. "Every time you people lose a paper clip somewhere, I end up running my ass off at a moment's notice. I just don't think you realize that I take two weeks to come up to peak."

He sipped his water and pushed the rice away from him. It was not natural unhusked rice, but the mass-produced imitation guaranteed not to cling to other grains and to stand up fresh within one minute of cooking. One time-saving minute. It also had the nutritive value of spit. He would be as well off eating cotton candy.

The water was also a chemical concoction of which one ingredient was water. He remembered a line he'd read once: "The water contained all the necessary nutrients including chow mein." Chiun's teaching had become part of him and water was important, even if he sometimes longed for a Seagram's Seven and beer chaser and on a very rare occasion allowed himself a cigarette.

The waiter asked if there was anything wrong with the rice. Dr. Smith answered for Remo. "No, the rice is fine. Just peculiar taste of some people."

"Like wanting to see tomorrow," mumbled Remo, glancing at the arriving and departing planes.

When the waiter had left, Remo, without taking his eyes off a 747 that seemed suspended in air just above the ground, like a horizontal hotel that hadn't decided it should fall, said:

"What is it this time?"

Dr. Smith leaned forward across the table. He whispered: "The United States government is for sale."

Remo turned back to the table, eyed the water balefully, contemplated the edge of a shiny brown roll, then said laconically, "So what else is new?"

"I mean for sale on the world markets."

"Oh, it's going international. Well, that's been the way for the last quarter of a century," Remo suggested.

"I mean," said Smith, "that someone is offering control of the key departments of the United States government for sale. The defense department, national security, treasury department, espionage systems. For sale."

"What can I say? Buy."

"Be serious," said Smith.

"I am, damn you. I am serious. I'm serious when I take off some guy's head. Some guy I never knew. I'm serious when the only thing a person means to me is his move right or move left. I'm serious when I say it all doesn't really matter that much anymore and never mattered that much to begin with. And we were all pretty stupid to think it ever did."

Remo turned back to the airplanes, and added: "I've been thinking about this a long time, Smith. I'm through."

"Okay," said Smith. "Okay. Let's walk out of here. I want to tell you something."

"If you're going to try to remove me, don't bother," Remo said. "You can't."

"I wouldn't be foolish enough to try, Remo."

"Nonsense. You're loose enough to try anything when it comes to this country. You'd try to outswim a tidal wave. I ought to put you out right now and then see what triggers those computers at Folcroft try to pull."

"I just want to talk to you, Remo. I want to talk to you about a man named Clovis Porter."

"Clovis Porter?" said Remo, smirking. "You WASPs sure do have a way with names."

"You may be a WASP yourself, Remo."

"Probably. It'd be my luck. Clovis Porter? C'mon. I wouldn't tell a Clovis Porter story to a hooker with a whip. Clovis Porter?"

"Clovis Porter," said Smith. "Just let me tell you about him."

But he did not speak in the cab from the airport and it was only later as they walked along the streets of Washington, D.C., that Smith opened the file on Clovis Porter, even to the dissolution of the century-old Porter fortune.

"You see, Porter invested his life's fortune to find out just what was going on. Like some other men you've known, he thought America was worth not only his fortune but his life."

The two white men crossed the invisible line into Washington's black ghetto, a line not marked by deteriorating houses but by a growing absence of Caucasians, a border that contracted with the sun and expanded with the dark. A few people looked from their windows, startled to see two white men strolling through their neighborhood as if the sun were noon-high.

Remo kicked a beer can.

"So that was Porter," Smith said. "And that was MacCleary. You remember MacCleary?"

"Yes, very much."

"He believed America was worth a life. Mine, yours, his own," Smith said.

"Where does it stop?" Remo asked.

"Where did it stop for MacCleary?" Smith asked.

"Where you killed him," he said, answering his own question. "And he knew why you had to do it."

Remo placed a hand on Smith's shoulder and Smith looked up, a parched face mirroring his parched life. Remo's first assignment had been to kill MacCleary, the man who had recruited him, because MacCleary had been injured and, under drugs, he might have talked.

"I never killed MacCleary," Remo said. "I never killed him."

"What?"

"I couldn't. He begged me to and I couldn't do it. So he did it himself."

"Oh, no," Smith said.

"Yeah. And when I read about it, I figured okay, one assignment. For MacCleary's stupidity."

"I didn't know," said Smith and his voice wavered. "I didn't know."

"Yeah, well, one assignment became another and then another and what with Chiun's training, it was like I was meant to do this and nothing else. And then it became like punching a time clock. You know what I feel when I kill a man?"

"No," said Smith softly.

"Not a damned thing. Half the time I'm thinking about my technique. And they're human lives, and I just don't care."

"What's bothering you?"

"I'm telling you, dammit."

"No, you're not. Why all of a sudden now?"

"It's not all of a sudden. It's all of an accumulation."

"The new faces bother you, don't they?"

"You better believe it," Remo said.

"We'll bring you back close next time."

"Unless you tell the surgeon to slip because I've suddenly become highly unreliable."

"Unless I do," said Smith.

From the streetlight above, insects swirled a storm of buzzing life as Remo said, "I could go through an operation like that without anesthesia."

"I imagine you could."

"I know that Chiun is one of your triggers if you push the button against me."

"That's obvious. He's a professional," Smith said.

"Even that's more of a reason than I have," Remo said.

Smith propped his briefcase against a streetlight and flipped it open. Remo made an imperceptible set, ready to move if necessary. But Smith brought out only a tape recorder.

"I want you to listen to this," he said and flipped the switch.

The next voice was Clovis Porter.

And on that corner in Washington, D.C., under streetlights swimming with bugs, Remo heard an Iowa farmer say good-bye to his wife for the last time — good-bye to the wife he loved, because he loved his country more.

And Remo finally said, "Okay, you sonofabitch. Just one more."

Six

It was enough to make Philander Jackson give up mugging. It certainly was enough to make Piggy Smith and Dice Martin stop walking again and to make Boom Boom Bosely look for some form of employment which did not require the use of his hands.

Not that Boom Boom had ever held a job, and but for brief stints at the Auto-Quicki-Car-Shine, neither had Philander, Piggy, or Dice.

Now they all had a legitimate excuse for welfare. This did not comfort them in the emergency room of the Fairoaks Hospital where Piggy blamed Philander for gross stupidity by calling him mother this and mother that. Dice was not about to blame anyone. He had not quite seen what had happened. And Boom Boom was too preoccupied with groaning to blame anyone. If one could decipher his unintelligible mumblings, he might be led to believe that Boom Boom was blaming his wrists for hurting so much.

This was unfair to Boom Boom's wrists. Any wrists would hurt after the bones had been crushed into blood-soaked pumice.

But how was Philander to know? It had looked too good to be true. Two white men standing alone in the heart of the ghetto just before the bars were closing, and those two honkies were grooving on a tape recording of some cat talking funny, real funny.

And Philander, Piggy, Dice, and Boom Boom jiving cool and out of bread, man. Those two Charlies were a gift, man. A stone gift. Especially the skinny old one.

So Philander, Piggy, Boom Boom, and Dice, just cool, man, made the scene.

"Evenin', folks," Philander had said.

The skinny old Charlie glanced briefly at the crew, then back to the other dude he was rapping with.

"Ah said evenin' folks," Philander said.

"Evenin'," said Boom Boom, Dice, and Piggy.

"Uh, yes. Good evening," said the skinny honky with a briefcase. He didn't look shook at all.

"You all got a penny?" asked Philander.

And then the younger honky said:

"Go suck a watermelon."

"Wha' you say?"

"I said, go suck a watermelon. This isn't the welfare office."

"Oh, you come down real badass, man. You know where you is?"

"The monkey house at the zoo?"

"You grin, you in. That gonna mean grape to you, Charlie."

Then the older Charlie spoke. "Look. We don't want any trouble. Just leave us alone and you won't be harmed."

Piggy laughed. Dice grinned. Philander chuckled and Boom Boom brought out the little piece he had been packing. The pistol gleamed in the streetlight as if the metal were sweating.

"Ah kill a honky as soon as ah look at him," said Boom Boom.

"He a badass. A real badass," said Philander confidentially to the two Charlies.

"Ah kill them mothers 'fore they was born," said Boom Boom. "Ah waste them good."

"Better pump some grape his way, boys," said Philander. "He a mean mother."

And then, surprisingly, the younger white man spoke to the older as if Philander, Piggy, Dice, and Boom Boom with his piece were not there.

"All right, it's settled. The general will be first tonight and then I'll check with you in the rooming. I'm bringing Chiun up. I don't feel as sharp as I should."

"All right," said the older Charlie. "But now I imagine you understand why it's so important we are involved in this. Everyone else has been compromised because they're known."

"I've got bad news for you," said the younger honky. Boom Boom looked at Philander and shrugged. Dice and Piggy both pointed index fingers at their heads and circled them indicating the honkies were crazy. Standing in the middle of Washington's Harlem, four bloods with a piece looking to waste them, and these two loose ends were talking compromise this and set-up that as if they were going to make it out in one piece.

"Bad news," said the younger honky. "Somebody knows something. I was jumped in Miami. We're not totally clean anymore; we've been tapped somewhere along the line."

The old geezer put his hand to his mouth. "There's only one other person who . . ."

"That's right," said the young looney.

"My God," said the old skinny honky. "I hope it doesn't mean what I think it means."

Then Boom Boom mumbled a curse and pushed the revolver in the younger honky's face.

"You guys bugged about something, man," said Boom Boom. "Maybe I ain't coming down too clear. But this is a holdup."

"Okay," said the younger one. "How much you want?" Sweet as you please, he said that.

"How much you got?" asked Boom Boom.

"I'll give you guys a hundred apiece. And we'll call it even."

"Fifty," said the old honky with the briefcase.

"Make it a hundred. Why not," said the younger screwball. "Fifty doesn't go far these days."

"A hundred here, a hundred there. It all mounts up. Make it seventy-five."

"Okay. Seventy-five," said the younger honky.

"Can ah get involved in this heah thing?" said Boom Boom, waving the gun wider because obviously someone was missing something. "This is mah holdup and ah got a right to say what ah's gonna get."

"Seventy-five be all right with you?" asked the younger honky.

"No," said Boom Boom.

"No way," said Piggy and Dice. "We wants it all. Everything you got. That briefcase too."

"Well, sorry," said the younger honky and then it all happened very fast. Boom Boom was shrieking and jumping up and down, shaking his hands, which flopped as though attached to his arms only by loose rubber bands.

Piggy and Dice were on the ground, their legs stiff, and then Philander thought he saw the flash of a white hand in the streetlight, but he could not be perfectly sure. He was still seeing the flash come at him when someone told him he was now in the hospital emergency room and everything was all right.

Seven

Mrs. Vance Withers did not tell the police everything. Yes, she awoke during the night to find her husband dead in bed. No face. It was horrible. No. She had heard nothing. Nothing.

"You mean to tell us, lady, that somebody did that to your husband and you didn't hear a thing?"

The detective sat on her new divan, his $75 suit on her $1,800 leather divan, and dared to speak gruffly to her as he penciled things into a little notebook. He was only a sergeant or something.

"Does your colonel know you speak like this to people?"

"I'm a cop, lady, not a soldier."

"Well, General Withers was a soldier," said Mrs. Withers icily. She had thrown on a flimsy pink something and now wished she had worn something heavier. Like a suit. And perhaps conducted the interview on the porch. She did not like the sergeant being so familiar. It was akin to disrespect for the departed General Vance Withers.

Two white-clad attendants removed the general through the living room on a wheeled stretcher. A white sheet covered what was left of his head.

"Yes, ma'am. We are aware the general was a soldier."

"I sense a certain disrespect in your voice, Sergeant. There is insubordination in manner, you know."

"Lady, I am not a soldier."

"That should be apparent to anyone."

"You are the only one, Mrs. Withers, who was with the general when that terrible thing happened. I'm afraid that makes you a suspect."

"Don't be absurd. General Withers was a four-star general and a good candidate for five stars. Why should I kill him?"

"Rank is not the only relationship, lady. Like sometimes there are other things between men and women, you know?"

"You really aren't a soldier, are you?"

"You still claim you heard nothing?"

"That is correct," said Mrs. Vance Withers. She pulled her pink nightdress tighter around her shoulders. She was an attractive woman with the sexuality of incipient middle age, a last longing fling of a body no longer designed to bear children.

Only — Mrs. Withers had a little secret. But she had no intention of sharing it with an enlisted man. So, she listened to the grubby police corporal or whatever he called himself and remembered just a few hours before, thinking she heard something and turning in bed. And then she felt those delicious hands quiet her eyes gently, just the fingertips on her eyelids, and then the strong but velvet-smooth hands awakened her body until, almost as if electrically shocked, she was alive with desire, throbbing, demanding, needing, and then there was fulfillment as she had never dared dream fulfillment. Shrieking in sudden and complete ecstasy.

"Vance. Vance. Vance."

And the magnificent hands were still there, to keep her eyes gently shut and in blissful satisfaction. Complete, she returned to sleep, and awoke again only when she thought she felt Vance salivating on her shoulder.

And she turned and her husband's pillow was a mass of blood. What she had felt was his blood.

"Oh," she had said. "Oh, no. No."

And then she phoned the police and here she was, somehow not totally distressed. Although Vance was destined for a fifth star. She just knew it. What a way to die, on the threshold of your fifth star. She grieved with her husband's memory.

"I'm going to ask you again, Mrs. Withers. Your husband's head was literally taken off and you heard nothing? Not even a scream?"

"No," she said. "I heard nothing. One cannot hear hands move."

"How do you know it was hands?"

Hmmm, she thought, that was a mistake.

"Well, lady," said the policeman, "don't think we think human hands could do that."

Mrs. Withers shrugged. These enlisted men were so stupid really.

Eight

There were definite advantages to being the confidential secretary to a banker from the centuries-old house of Rapfenberg. The salary was good. There was a lot of travel. There was a sense of excitement and the feeling of being in on important things — even if, sometimes, they were a little too complicated to understand.

It was a sweet job, especially for a twenty-four-year-old American girl who had originally come to Zurich to ski. Eileen Hamblin told herself that again, as she tried to convince herself that the last three months had not really been so bad.

There had been no traveling and that, she realized, was the source of her discomfort. She had been virtually chained to this awful desk for three months because Mr. Amadeus Rentzel had work to do in Zurich and that had, for the very first time, introduced in her the suspicion that banking might be dull. Just plain dull. Banking, she thought in a very un-Swiss-like manner, could be just a boring pain in the ass.

If she had been a better secretary, she might have tried to learn something about banking, finance, and monetary policy, so she could perhaps share in the excitement others seemed to find in them. Gold was gold and silver was silver. They were used for jewelry. But money was used to pay the rent. She could find no possible relationship between the paper currency she used at the grocery store and somebody's pile of gold buried in some fort somewhere.

Mr. Rentzel had tried to explain, but it was useless. And now he no longer tried. And for the past three months, he had been different somehow, spending more time at his desk, always deep in charts on cash and reserves and gold flow.

She remembered the day it had started, how he had come out of his office and said, "Gold stocks are dropping on the New York Stock Exchange."

"That's nice," she said.

"Nice?" he said. "It's awful."

"Is there anything we can do about it?"

"Not a damn thing," he said, disappearing back into his office.

From that day on, her first job every day was to begin checking gold prices on major stock exchanges around the world. In the last month, they had been going up and so had Mr. Rentzel's spirits.

Suddenly Mr. Rentzel became extremely popular. Formerly, he would travel all over the world — with Eileen — to see clients. But now the clients were coming to him. A regular United Nations in the last month. Orientals. Russians, even.

There was another one today. His card had read "Mister Jones." Eileen had allowed herself a very small, very controlled smile. The man had an accent like Ludwig Von Drake, and if he were Mr. Jones, she was Jacqueline Onassis.

The man known as Mr. Jones was inside Mr. Rentzel's office now, nervously fingering the catches on a black leather attache case, which was fastened to his arm with an old-fashioned pair of handcuffs.

"I am glad your nation has decided to bid," Rentzel told the man.

Rentzel was tall and sandy-haired and looked younger than his fifty years. He wore conservative clothing, not because he liked it but because a banker could wear nothing else. He was a very good banker.

The man he addressed — Mr. Jones of the business card — was a small, fat man with a bald head and thick, horn-rimmed eyeglasses. He watched Rentzel without speaking, with slightly less animation than that shown by a subway rider reading an overhead advertisement.

"Of course, the bombing demonstration at St. Louis was very impressive, was it not?" Rentzel said.

Jones grunted into the silence. Then there was more silence. Then Jones said, "I have the money here."

"In dollars?"

"Yes."

"And you understand the rules?"

"Please repeat them," Jones said and reached for a pen in the inside pocket of his ill-fitting blue serge suit.

Rentzel raised a hand in a traffic-stopping gesture. "Please. Nothing in writing." Jones slowly withdrew his empty hand while Rentzel walked around the desk and sat in his chair, facing Jones across the wide expanse of walnut.

Without waiting, he began to talk. "Your two million dollars will be held by me as a good-faith deposit on behalf of your country. The bidding will be conducted seven days from today in the New York offices of the Villebrook Equity Associates."

"I have never heard of them," Jones said.

"That is the proof of their quality," Rentzel said with a smile. "They are bankers, not public relations men for themselves. At any rate, the bidding will be conducted there by me. Each nation will be allowed one bid and one bid only. The minimum price is, as you know, one billion dollars. In gold. The highest bid over one billion dollars wins."

"One billion dollars," Jones said. "It is an awesome figure."

"What is for sale is also awesome," Rentzel said. "Control of the government of the most powerful nation in the history of the world." He went on. "By the way, you should know the competition. Besides your own country, I expect bids from Russia and China, Italy, France, and Great Britain. And oh, from Switzerland, too."

"You Swiss always were adventurers," Jones said with a chuckle.

"And you Germans always were fascinated by the possibility of controlling others. Oh, the bids must be in writing and sealed. All unsuccessful bidders will have their good-faith deposits returned to them by me. I will, of course, give you a receipt for it now."

"It must be interesting to be able to sell a government," Jones said. "Interesting, that is, for the person doing it. It would seem the only person who could do it would be the president," he added somewhat clumsily.

"Who is doing it is unimportant," Rentzel said. "The fact is that my client can do it. The incident with the nuclear weapon on St. Louis showed that. Tomorrow, there will be another incident. It will involve the Central Intelligence Agency. When you hear of it, you will recognize it. The power to accomplish such things will be yours if you are the successful bidder."

"But one billion dollars in gold? Do you realize how much gold that is?"

"In the neighborhood of one thousand tons," Rentzel said. "Don't worry. In Switzerland, we have the facilities for storing it. And the trust of our client."

"We may not bid," Jones said sullenly, simply out of dislike for this man who knew all the answers.

"It would be your loss," Rented said. "The other nations plan to. One can tell by the fact that gold mining stocks are moving up in value on their stock exchanges."

He smiled. Jones knew that Rentzel had seen the price of gold stocks climbing in Germany too. Rentzel realized that Germany was already beginning to stockpile the gold needed to back up their bid.

"Well, we shall see," he said lamely.

With his left hand, he quickly unlocked the handcuff on his wrist and placed the attache case on the desk before Rentzel. "Do you wish to . . . ?"

"No, that's not necessary," Rentzel said. "In matters like this, we make no mistakes."

He rose and shook hands with Mr. Jones, who quickly left. Rentzel opened the briefcase and looked at the neat piles of thousand-dollar bills. Two million dollars.

With the nonchalance of the professional banker, he left the briefcase open on his desk and stepped into the outer office. Jones had gone. His secretary was cleaning her nails.

She looked up and was disappointed when he said, "Pay close attention to mining stock prices in Paris and in London." Then he smiled, and said, "And make us reservations for a flight to New York Sunday night."

Without waiting for an answer, he turned and walked back into his office. He could not see the huge smile that illuminated her face.

Great, she thought. New York. Banking could really be fun, after all.

On the other hand, she could not see the smile on Rentzel's face. The CIA incident, he thought. After that, all the countries will get in line to bid.

Nine

"Good evening, Burton," sang Dr. Lithia Forrester.

An athletic man on the verge of going to pot stood in the doorway in sandals, slacks, and open-necked shirt. He had a deep tan, even through his receding hairline.

His eyebrows narrowed and two dark, puffing bags under his watery blue eyes stood like pedestals beneath statues to the great god tension. He picked at his temple.

"Uh, yeah. Good evening."

"Won't you come in?"

"Of course, I'm going to come in, Dr. Forrester. What do you think I'm here for?"

Dr. Forrester smiled warmly and shut the door behind Burton Barrett, an operations chief of the Central Intelligence Agency, recuperating from the rigors of the quiet, thankless pressure of working one's ass off in a void. Reporting to people he did not know. Having other people he did not know report to him. Situation reports, which came from places he did not know and went to other places he did not know. This for fifteen years — then he had snapped. And now he was being mended at the Human Awareness Laboratories. Prize patient number one.

"Won't you sit down, Burton?"

"No, Dr. Forrester, I'm going to stand on my head, thank you. I like standing on my head."

Lithia Forrester sat down behind her desk and crossed her legs. Burton Barrett plumped himself down into a deep leather couch, not looking at Doctor Forrester but staring up, out into the sky. He did not focus on the stars or even the glimmering reflection of the inside lights on the dome. His was a concentrated not-staring, and what he specifically was not staring at was Lithia Forrester.

"Well, this is it, as if you give a shit," he said.

"You're rather hostile tonight, Burton. Any special reason?"

"No, just run-of-the-mill hostile. You know, in the morning you're hungry and in the evening you're hostile."

"Is it something to do with a need, Burton?"

"Need? I don't have needs. I'm Burton Barrett from the Main Line and I'm a WASP and I'm rich and I'm handsome and therefore I don't have needs and feelings. I have no sympathies, no loves, no emotions. Just strengths and greed and, of course, controls." Burton Barrett whistled nervously and softly after he said this. He drummed on the couch.

"Needs?" he repeated. "No, I don't have needs. Burton Barrett has no needs. Burton Barrett has no friends. Burton Barrett needs no friends. Sexy Burton Barrett is in the Central Intelligence Agency. That's sexy, right?"

"No, that's not sexy, Burton. You know that. And I know it."

"I have such a sexy job, it took me weeks to be relieved of duty, then cleared to come here to you."

"That's not unusual for your line of work."

"Have you ever spent hours discussing your possible emotional problems with an FBI agent? An FBI agent named Bannon? And then waiting for him to check me out and then to recommend a psychologist. I mean, that's something — Bannon! Or am I not allowed to be prejudiced against the Irish? I forget who you're allowed to be prejudiced against. It keeps changing."

"We're not dealing with what's bothering you, Burton."

"This is my last day, as you know."

"Yes, I know."

"I'm not cured."

"Well, cured is a very relative term."

"That helps me a lot."

"You'll be able to come back regularly. At least once a week."

"Once a week is not enough, Dr. Forrester."

"We must do the best we can with what we have."

Burton Barrett clenched his fists. "Oh, dammit, Lithia, I love you. I love you. And don't give me that crap about it being normal to love your therapist. I've been in therapy before and I never, never loved Dr. Filbenstein."

"Let's deal with your needs for love. Dr. Filbenstein is a man. You're heterosexual. I'm a woman."

"*No tiddypoo?* Really, Lithia, you're really a woman. I dream about you. Do you know I dream about having you?"

"Let's talk about your love needs. When was the first time you felt your needs were not being met?"

Burton Barrett stretched back onto the couch and closed his eyes. Back he went to the nurse, his mother, his father. His red wagon. He liked his red wagon.

It was a good wagon. You could get a good head start with a foot push. You could whack it into the fat maid's balloon legs. The maid's legs were like pier pilings. Her name was Flo. She would scream and yell.

Burton Barrett was told never to ram the wagon into the maid again. So he did.

Then he was told if he did that again, his wagon would be taken away. So he did, and it was.

And Burton Barrett cried and wouldn't eat lunch and promised if he ever got his wagon back again, he would never ever ram the maid with it again. Never. He promised.

So he got his wagon back and rammed the maid again. She hit him and was fired. He felt bad about that. And he did not complain when the wagon was taken from him, for good that time.

"Why did you ram her with your wagon?" Lithia Forrester asked.

"I don't know. Why do people climb mountains? Because she was there. Anyway, what does my wagon have to do with it? I'm going back to my shitty job in a shitty office in a shitty city and dammit, Lithia, I love you. And that's my problem."

"You love me because I represent something to you."

"You represent, Lithia, the most beautiful woman I've ever seen."

"Was your mother beautiful?"

"No. She was my mother."

"That doesn't preclude her being beautiful."

"In my family it does. We all marry ugly women. Me too. If it weren't for my affair with that artist in New York, I'd go nuts."

"Do you think going to bed with me would help you, Burton?"

Burton Barrett sat up on the couch as though goosed with a cattle prod. He looked over at Dr. Lithia Forrester. She was smiling. Her lips were moist.

"Do you mean it?"

"Do you think I mean it?"

"I don't know. You said it."

"What I said was, do you think it would help?"

"Yes," said Burton Barrett very honestly.

Dr. Lithia Forrester nodded.

"Then we're going to make love?"

"I didn't say that."

"Dammit, Lithia, why do you keep coming back with these stupid cutesy answers that don't say anything. If anyone else were that smartass with me, outside, I'd smash them in the face. I really would. Right in the face. Now, let's deal with my aggressions. Well, sweetie, fuck my aggressions. Deal with this."

And with that, Burton Barrett, regional director for the intelligence network of the most powerful nation on earth, unzipped his fly.

"I fully intend to deal with that," Lithia Forrester said. "I fully intend to. But first you're going to have to do a few things."

Burton Barrett blinked, grinned, then, in surprise and shame, he zipped up his fly.

"You didn't have to do that, Burton, but we'll deal with that later. First, we're going to have a little drink and then I want you to hum a little tune with me."

"That sounds silly," he said.

"Those are my requirements. If you really want to sleep with me, you'll meet them."

"What's the tune?" asked Burton Barrett.

"It goes da da da da dum da dum dum da da da da dum dum," she said.

"Hey, I know that song," he said. "It's from the movie . . ."

"Exactly," she said. "Now hum it with me," she said, as she stood and walked slowly toward the couch where Burton Barrett had again stretched full-length.

He was still humming the catchy little melody the next afternoon when he walked into the National Press Club headquarters in

Washington, D.C., jumped onto a stage and told the assembled press of the world that he had a few things to say.

And then he announced that the United States government had seven ex-Nazis on its CIA payroll in South America. He mentioned their names, their home addresses in South America, and also the names under which they had been sought for years by the Israelis.

He promised the press photographs of the men.

He also listed the names of four agents working undercover in Cuba. And just to convince the reporters that he knew what he was talking about, he tossed his identification badge to a reporter from the *Washington Post*, sitting in the front row.

"Why are you disclosing this? Have you been ordered to?" asked the reporter.

"Why does anyone do anything? I just felt like it, that's all."

Then Burton Barrett said, "Look, check out what I told you. It's all true. But I've got to be going, because they'll be after me soon."

He jumped off the stage and walked leisurely through the audience, ignoring the reporters who tried to question him, carefully humming to himself a catchy little tune.

Burton Barrett was right. The CIA was after him within minutes. They did not find him in his office in Langley, Virginia, or in his small apartment, nor back at Human Awareness Laboratories.

He turned up after dark in one of the small reading rooms in the Washington public library's main building. He had bought a pack of leather thong shoelaces, and had tied them together into a long string. Then, he wet them, sopping wet, in a washroom sink. He wrapped the stretchy wet leather several times around his neck and tied it tightly with a knot. As the minutes passed, the leather dried and began to contract. As it contracted, it cut deeper and deeper into Burton Barrett's throat.

Witnesses reported later that he did not seem to mind. He just sat there, humming to himself, reading a large illustrated book about Mary Poppins, and then, sometime after 4:30 P.M., he fell forward onto the table, dead.

Burton Barrett's self-strangulation had repercussions. It was front-page news in the papers of the world. The United States received strongly worded notes of protest from both Israel and the Latin

American country that housed the seven ex-Nazis. Four U.S. agents in Cuba were killed.

In Zurich, a Swiss banker from the House of Rapfenberg received word that yes, France was definitely interested in bidding.

Burton Barrett's life story went into the computers at the CURE headquarters at Folcroft, and it was mixed and matched against Clovis Porter and General Dorfwill, and back out came a sentence:

"Check Human Awareness Laboratories for possible link."

The people who would destroy America had opened a door. Through it would walk the Destroyer.

Ten

Remo had just picked up the telephone to call Smith, when there was a knock on his hotel room door. He put the phone back down and was about to yell "Come in, it's open," when the door flung open and Chiun stood there. Behind him were two bellhops and Chiun's luggage. Three large steamer trunks.

Chiun could travel for a year with a manila envelope if he had to. If he didn't have to, he could fill two baggage cars. So when Remo had phoned Miami to tell Chiun to follow, he had limited the luggage to three trunks. No more.

Chiun left as soon as the soap operas were over, not even waiting to play his special TV tapes of the simultaneous programs. He would wait, he told Remo, until he reached Washington.

Remo had thanked him, knowing Chiun considered this truly a sacrifice.

Because of American stupidity, as Chiun put it, all the good shows ran at one time, so that a person could not watch them all. To compensate for the gross obtuseness of American television functionaries, Chiun therefore would watch *Dr. Lawrence Walters, Psychiatrist*, while on two portable machines he would tape *Edge of Dawn* and *As the Planet Revolves*.

Chiun allowed the bellboys to precede him into Remo's hotel suite. Remo stepped away from the phone, reached into his slacks pocket, and unpeeled two single dollar bills. This would ease the departure of the bellboys. Chiun never tipped. He considered "the bearing of loads" a hotel service, not to be unduly recompensed. In lieu of a tip, he would grade the bellboys on their chores from inadequate to good. He had given one good in his lifetime and many inadequates. Today

53

the two bellboys got adequates. They stared at the frail Oriental in disbelief. Remo waved the money at them and they left shaking their heads.

"Throw money hither. Throw money yon. Spend, spend, spend until pauperdom. You, Remo, are truly an American."

The voice was mild but it was Chiun's ultimate insult. Next worst was "you are a white man."

When Remo was first in training, a basic training that had never before been seen outside Chiun's village of Sinanju, Korea, Chiun had explained to him the formation of the world and its peoples.

"When God created man," Chiun had said, "he put a lump of clay in the oven. And when he took it out, he said, 'It is underdone. This is no good. I have created a white man.' Then he put another lump of clay in the oven, and to compensate for his error, he left it in longer. When he took it out, he said, 'Oh, I have failed again. I have left it in too long. This is no good. I have created a black man.' And then he put another lump of clay in the oven, this time a superior clay, molded with more care and love and integrity, and when he took it out, he said: 'Oh, I have done it just right. I have created the yellow man.'

"And then to this man in whom he was pleased he gave a mind. To the Chinese, he gave lust and dishonesty. To the Japanese, he gave arrogance and greed. To the Koreans, he gave honesty, courage, integrity, discipline, beauty of thought, heart, and wisdom. And because he had given them so much, he said, 'I shall also give them poverty and conquerors because they have been given more already than any other man on earth. They are truly the perfect people in my sight, and in their wonderfulness, I am well pleased.'"

Remo was still recovering physically from his electrocution. He had been only half listening but he had caught the direction of the lesson.

"You're Korean, aren't you?"

"Yes," said the smiling old man. "How did you know?"

"I guessed," Remo said.

The lesson, in all its variations, had been repeated many times during Remo's training all those years ago. Once when Remo had done a particularly difficult exercise without flaw, Chiun had shrieked, "Excellent."

"Excellent, Little Father?" Remo had said in pleasant surprise.

And recovering, Chiun had said: "Yes. For a white man, excellent. For a Korean, good."

"Dammit," Remo had said, "I know I can take just about any Korean around, I'd say almost everyone, except you."

"How many Koreans do you know, oh open-mouthed shouter of an American white man?"

"Well, just you."

"And you can defeat me?"

"Not you, probably."

"Probably? Shall we find out?"

"No."

"You are afraid of hurting me?"

"Well, blow it out your ears," Remo had said.

"Here, we see American logic. You are sure you can defeat any Korean except one. And that one is the only Korean you know. And in response to his efforts and teachings to try to make something of the undercooked lump of clay which is you, he receives 'Blow it out your ears.' Oh, perfidy."

"I'm sorry, Little Father."

"Do not be sorry afterwards. Be sorry before. Then you will be a man who uses his mind to make his way instead of to repair it."

Remo had bowed and Chiun had said: "You can defeat any Korean, except probably one."

"Thank you, Little Father."

"For what? You thank me for an observation that my skills at teaching are so powerful that I can even impart some of them to a white man. I will accept your admiration, not your thanks."

"You have always had my admiration, Little Father."

Chiun had bowed.

And Remo had never let Chiun know that when Chiun saved him from the Chinese conspirators, Remo had, in a mind that functioned even while he was near death, heard Chiun scream in his search for Remo: "Where is my child whom I have made with my heart and my mind and my will?"

Remo never let him know he had heard, because that knowledge brought to light would have embarrassed Chiun, exposing that he now thought of Remo as a Korean.

Remo picked up the phone while Chiun was unpacking. First out came the TV tape players and then, from the folds of his golden robe, Chiun removed the tapes of *Edge of Dawn* and *As the Planet Revolves.*

Chiun did not trust the tapes to luggage. Luggage could be lost. He plugged in his portable tape receiver deck and then, sitting down on one of the trunks that blocked passage in the suite, he began intently watching Laura Wade disclose to Brent Wyatt that she feared the famous nuclear physicist Lance Rex would suffer a nervous breakdown if he discovered that his Tricia Bonnecut really loved the Duke of Ponsonby who had just inherited the main salmon and silk factories in Mulville.

Remo heard the phone being picked up at the other end. "Seven-four-four," Smith said.

"Open line," said Remo.

"Yes, of course. You've read in the papers about our friend in the library?"

"Yes."

"He was part of it too." Smith changed his tone, becoming conspiratorial. "I would think you need a rest. A very good place to rest is the Human Awareness Laboratories, about fifty miles outside Baltimore. Go there and rest up. Register as a patient. They might be interested in having Mr. Donaldson as a patient."

"Anything I should specialize in?"

"I imagine you might jump the line," Smith said.

Remo grunted and hung up. Jumping the line meant that Remo should allow himself to be the target of attack, then follow the attack back to its source and then kill the source. It was effective and dangerous, an easy way to get killed. Still, an open telephone line in Washington, D.C., was not the worst way to attract attention. Besides, Remo was already a target for someone, as the Silver Creek Country Club had proved.

Remo began to strip for his exercises, which would begin after *As the Planet Revolves.* He would wear a blue uniform today. The colors meant something to Chiun, if not to Remo, and Chiun always seemed to be in a better humor when Remo wore blue.

Eleven

Chiun didn't even turn away from the television when the knock came. Remo was showering.

"Will you get it, Chiun?" said Remo, throwing a towel around his waist and puddling out of the shower stall, already knowing that his comfort versus *As the Planet Revolves* was a certain loser.

He hopped a bed, and, making dark wet marks on the gray rug, made it to the door.

"Yes," he called out.

"FBI," came the voice from the other side of the door.

"I'm showering."

"We'll only be a minute," came the voice.

Remo glanced back at Chiun. The master had been restive lately and Remo didn't want people in the room when the Master of Sinanju was involved in Mrs. Vera Halpers confessing to Wayne Walton that Bruce Barton and Lance Rerton may have spent Thanksgiving in a motel with Lysetta Hanover and Patricia Tudor.

That interruption could end up with eye sockets on the wall.

Remo opened the door a crack. "Look," he whispered. "See, I'm wet. Can you come back in an hour?"

There was a group of three men, all wearing brown snap-brimmed hats, shined cordovans, gray lightweight summer suits, white shirts, and conservative ties. They were all clean-shaven and not one of them appeared to have a cavity or a tooth defect.

It had amused Remo that this uniform, this sparkling advertisement of membership in the Federal Bureau of Investigation, was called plainclothes. If they wanted to be inconspicuous, they might have done better in an increasingly permissive society by being more permissive with themselves.

As Chiun had said, "When the fish climb trees, you do not go swimming to hide as a fish."

The apparent leader of the group offered a little two-piece wallet device, which exposed an FBI identity card in plastic. It was his face, showing roundish, somewhat aging, symmetrical features. A smile could have made it a nice face.

It was not a nice face now. "'Can we come in?"

"Get a warrant," said Remo.

"We have one," said the man, whose name on the card was Supervisor Bannon. Remo shrugged.

"Okay, but be quiet," he said and opened the door. The three men entered. The two behind Bannon masked tension. Remo could see it in their eyes. They took off their hats and opened the distance between them, almost making the base of a triangle for Bannon's point.

They were watching Bannon more closely than Remo. Absently, they showed their cards to Remo, who saw they were a Winarsky and a Tracy and they were duly authorized to do whatever duly authorized people were authorized to do.

Which didn't help Remo's goose bumps as he stood with a towel wrapping his groin. He was slightly shorter than the men, and his body would not necessarily disclose his skills. Undressed, he looked like a relatively healthy tennis player. Bannon looked like an ex-tackle for the Rams. The other two could have been tennis players, twenty pounds on the wrong side of six-love. Bannon sat down in a soft chair, his hat still on his head.

Winarsky and Tracy eyed Chiun. Remo shut the door. Bannon looked deep into his own navel. Remo saw Tracy and Winarsky exchange glances.

"Oriental," said Supervisor Bannon. "The man is Oriental."

"Shhh," came the voice from Chiun who sat slide-rule straight and quiet, poised two body lengths across the gray carpeting from Supervisor Bannon. Remo patted downward in the air, indicating that Supervisor Bannon should lower his tone.

"Oriental," said Supervisor Bannon.

Winarsky said to Remo: "You're Remo Donaldson, correct?"

"Right," said Remo.

"Remo Donaldson," said Bannon, looking up from his stomach. "Why did you kill those Special Forces people in Florida? Why did you kill General Withers? Why did you do those terrible things, Remo Donaldson?"

Remo shrugged and appeared confused. He looked to Winarsky and Tracy.

"We have reason to believe you may be connected with the death of some government people in Florida," Winarsky explained. "We want to talk to you about it."

"We want justice," said Supervisor Bannon. "That's what it's all about."

"Actually, Mr. Donaldson, justice is a function of the courts. We just gather information. We don't even indict anyone. We're just here for some information. The information you give us about yourself could just as easily clear you." Winarsky's voice was even and controlled. He looked directly at Remo.

Bannon looked to the ceiling. "Justice," he said. "If not justice, then what?"

Tracy leaned over and whispered into Bannon's ear. Bannon pushed at Tracy's shoulder and yelled: "I will not be interfered with. When you've spent as much time as I have rooting out injustice, then you can tell me how to interrogate a suspect. Then, Tracy, you can tell me about my job. Until then, Tracy, stand clear."

He turned to Remo. "Mr. Donaldson. Have you ever been to confession? Have you ever confessed your sins against the United States government? Against decency? Against democracy? Against the flag?"

"Sir," said Winarsky. "I think we had better leave Tracy here and you and I return to headquarters."

Bannon began to hum softly to himself, a tune that Remo couldn't make out. But he thought he had heard it before. Somewhere.

"We're not leaving anywhere," said Bannon. "We're not leaving our nation to injustice or . . ." Bannon stared up at the ceiling and then at Remo.

He hummed some more. He looked at Remo almost without seeing him. Then he slipped a .38-caliber snub-nosed revolver from a holster under his coat in a very nice motion. Much better than most FBI men drew. It was more relaxed than most men going for a gun, and thus its fluidity gave speed and command. Most likely the draw was an accident because Bannon had not looked that good when he walked in.

Bannon pointed the gun at Tracy, who instinctively raised his hands. The room was silent but for a woman on television extolling the virtues of the disposable diaper. According to the message, the diaper could not only keep baby dry but could make happy marriages. Since it was a commercial and since Chiun could sense the drawing of weapons — the sudden silence in the room tipping him off — he turned around to see what weapon was drawn on whom.

When he saw it was the fat meat-eater in the soft chair pointing a pistol at the overweight meat-eater standing, Chiun returned his gaze to the set and watched how Lemon Smart non-phosphate soap could make a wash sunshine fresh. Chiun had contempt for men who would use weapons at close range. As he had said: "You might as well push buttons. A child could kill like that."

"Sir," said Winarsky loudly.

"Shhh," said Chiun.

"Quiet the Oriental," said Bannon, pointing the gun at Tracy's stomach, then waving it toward Chiun. Tracy was nearest to Chiun.

"Wait," said Remo. "Don't go near the old man. Not now. Just stay where you are."

"Move, Tracy. Or I will put as big a hole into you as I plan to put into the injustice-maker, Remo Donaldson. I am judge and executioner, Donaldson. And my justice is keen."

"Sir," said Winarsky. "That's . . . that's not regulation." Remo could tell Winarsky knew it was weak when he said it. But then, in a crisis, man's ultimate values always surface, values he might not even know he had.

"Move, Tracy, or you are dead," said Bannon, whose gaze became vacant again as he hummed. What was that song? Remo could not make it out.

Bannon blinked. He focused. He brought his right hand flush to his hips, so the pistol could not be knocked away. A snub-nosed gun was perfect for this.

He pointed the little cannon, with the poised slug capable of making a grapefruit-sized gouge in flesh, at Tracy's stomach. Perspiration formed on Tracy's forehead. Remo saw him swallow.

Bannon was a quick one step and a simple stroke away. Remo could take the gun away whenever he wanted. But then Tracy began to move toward Chiun and Remo faced a new target line.

He tried. "Don't move," said Remo. "Don't go near that old man now. Don't go near him."

"Mister," said Agent Tracy. "There's a .38 being pointed at my stomach now and I can feel the slug in me already, so with your kind permission or without it, I am going to quiet this little old man."

"I've seen men survive bullet wounds," Remo said.

He could say no more before Tracy, in his nervousness, grabbed the wisp of white hair on Chiun's balding yellow head.

Tracy did this with his left hand as he kept his eye on Bannon, still believing the pistol was the major threat against his life. Probably he did not feel his wrist snap. First the wrist, and Tracy's body was going down into the floor as the golden-robed old man used its mass to rise on. Remo didn't even see the skull blow that killed Agent Tracy who had placed unreal fear in the efficacy of guns and paid the ultimate price for his miscalculation. The body bumped on the rug, dead before grounding.

Bannon was in pre-shoot, that just-about-a-second length of time between the recognition of danger and shooting. He did not have that just-about-a-second. A frail foot went through his right eye into his brain, which never got off its signal to squeeze the trigger.

Remo could see the foot because of the golden flowing robes floating violently around it. Winarsky moved a hand to his holster on his hip, a compendium of bad habits, exposing his heart, his chest, his throat, his head, as if he were posing to be killed. Winarsky undoubtedly thought reaching for a pistol like that was a good move. Maybe his best move. Remo would remember that white shirt, big and open and incredibly vulnerable. He would remember all motion stilled . . . the white open shirt . . . the hand moved away from any blocking action . . . the hand on the hip.

And the golden robes as Chiun seemed hung in the air, a red spot on the rug behind him where his big toe, having punctured an eyesocket, had touched the gray carpet after killing Bannon, and Chiun seemed poised in mid-air forever as if unable to decide in what spot he should kill Winarsky.

He narrowed the choices to one, and then it was over. Chiun had taken him with an off-angle, right-hand stroke just over the right temple above Winarsky's gun hand. Confronted with so many obvious targets and moves, he had taken an obscure angular attack.

Winarsky stood in his official FBI crouch, the one all agents are taught when they are taught how to draw their revolvers from their hips. He stood that way while a red splotch formed just above his right ear. He stood that way while he was dead.

When Agent Winarsky hit the floor, the Master of Sinanju was back at the problems of Middle America, being discussed by Middle America *ad infinitum*. Chiun, as he had often said, respected America's true art form.

Remo was left with two dead men on the floor and one in a chair.

He and Chiun might have to move rapidly. Then again, knowing how organizations worked, they might not have to move that fast at all.

Remo dialed FBI headquarters and asked for Supervisor Bannon, giving the name of a supervisor in Newark, New Jersey. Bannon was out to lunch, his secretary said.

"What about Agents Winarsky and Tracy?"

"Out to lunch with him."

"Do you know where I can reach him? It's urgent."

"Yes, the Plymouth Luncheonette. That's where he said he was going."

"Thank you," said Remo. So much for the trace from FBI headquarters. Remo dialed the desk clerk.

"Anyone been looking for me in the lobby? I'm expecting people."

"No," said the clerk.

So much for the FBI identifying themselves to the hotel clerk. Obviously, Bannon had been doing his own number outside regular channels. And he had done it without leaving a trace.

Remo moved the bodies to the bathtub, then dressed quickly in slacks, sports shirt, and soft Italian shoes. He wanted to look casual to attract less attention where he was going.

Just before he left, he said to the straight golden-robed body with the wisps of hair flowing down:

"Don't let anyone in, Chiun."

"Shhh," said the Master of Sinanju, who did not like beauty to be interrupted.

"You know, Chiun," yelled Remo, "if you weren't so magnificent, you'd be a shit." Then he slammed the door. Chiun never cleaned up his own bodies. Never.

The gardening-supply store assured the handsome young homeowner that even though his leaves were soggy, the Super Garb was not about to leak. It was tested, the owner assured the man who moved so smoothly, so it could hold — without tearing — 250 pounds.

"Give me three," said Remo.

The young homeowner moved so smoothly, did he ever participate in ballet?

"Wrap the Super Garbs," Remo said.

"Oh," said the owner, who frittered away to impose his will on a clerk who was overworked, over-abused, and heterosexual.

That afternoon, Remo learned that the Duralite extra-large suitcase was made of stanislucent polychromide.

"Thanks, give me three," said Remo to the clerk in the luggage shop.

"It also has the scratchproof, virtually scratchproof, exide exterior, with, and this is a prime feature, the new low-line snap buckle."

"Three," Remo said.

"It is guaranteed," said the clerk, "for eight years. That's an eight-year guarantee."

"Give me three before I grind you into a puppy biscuit remnant," Remo said, smiling.

"What did you say?" said the clerk who restrained himself from pounding the customer through the door because he knew he had a sale. Besides, if he had another incident at this store, then he would never again be able to get a job as a salesman.

"Three, please," said Remo. "Deliver them immediately," and he gave his room number at the hotel.

"Immediately," he said. "Or I won't pay for them."

"You have a half hour," he added smiling.

When the customer had left, the salesman said: "I hope I see him again. Preferably in a dark bar."

Did the gentleman want the valises insured?

"Of course," said Remo. "These valises hold very valuable possessions. Priceless. Insure them for $2,000 each."

Jewelry and things?

"No. Manuscripts. Priceless to me."

Oh, very nice. We will have our man pick them up in an hour in your hotel suite.

"Here," said Remo to the men picking up the three valises. "Here's a tenner for you and your partner. They're kind of heavy, so be careful with them. And don't disturb the little fellow watching television. Please."

Twelve

Remo had to take Chiun with him.

That was the first problem. Chiun had done it again, or rather, as Chiun explained it, he was minding his own business when it was done to him. Chiun, if you took literally what he said, was always minding his own business. Then he was abused, then a little something happened, and that was it.

"I would not expect it all to be understood by a man given to dilly-dallying as you did with those imbeciles before," Chiun said.

"Now let's go over this again," said Remo, packing his one valise with two throws of underwear and a neat folding of one extra suit, then moving on to Chiun's wardrobe.

"You were sitting peacefully in the downstairs restaurant, correct?"

"Correct."

Chiun motioned with one long finger that he wanted the white kimono folded outside in and the blue one folded inside out. Remo could have let Chiun pack his own luggage but they would not be out of the hotel for at least another day.

"And this person at the table next to you was talking about the Third World?"

"Correct."

"And you did not intrude yourself on their conversation?"

"Correct."

"Then what happened?"

"I will not be questioned like a child. The green robe is on top." Remo put the green robe on the bed for last.

"I've got to know for my report to Smith," Remo said.

"Of course. I had forgotten that I am dealing with a person who spies on me. I had forgotten that all I have taught you means ought. I had forgotten that truths that save your life are forgotten because you know them now and I, after all, do not rank in your wonderful organization. I do not even know the purpose of your organization. That is how little I am valued. I am just a poor teacher of the martial arts, a lowly, lowly servant. Put the sandals in a bag."

"May I remind you, Little Father, that it was you who told Smith I could function when I'm not at peak? I never risked your life," Remo said.

"If it makes you feel better to bring up old wounds, then indulge yourself. I am just a poor servant."

"Dammit, Chiun," said Remo, stuffing the first of eight pairs of sandals into the first of eight plastic bags. "When one of the most famous heavyweight contenders gets knocked on his ass by an eighty-year-old man, we have some explaining to do."

"No one saw it," Chiun said.

"They saw Ali Baba whatever-his-name-is go on his ass. They saw that."

"They did not see my hand, nor did the young gentleman, who, I might add, would probably make a much finer pupil than you. I could tell in his eyes. His basic balance was better. But Dr. Smith did not bring me a fine specimen like that to train. No, he brought me flotsam from the sewers of America, smelling of beef-eating and alcohol-drinking, his mind in constant haze, his balance never evoked, and from that nothing, I made a master. A true master." Then Chiun caught himself, and added quickly, "at least by American standards."

"All right. How did it happen?"

"I was concerned only with my own affairs when he cast unwarranted aspersions upon me. I ignored the insult because I wished no undue disturbance. I know your squeamishness and unwarranted fears."

"Then what happened?"

"I was insulted again."

"What did he say?"

"I do not wish to open old wounds."

"That was an hour and a half ago, Chiun, and the poor bastard is in the hospital. Not that long ago, Chiun. Now, what happened?"

66

Chiun stared from the window in regal silence.

"Your taping machines are not indestructible, Little Father," Remo said, "and I know you wouldn't lay out your own money to buy replacements."

"I have created a monster," sighed Chiun. "So be it. This is my punishment for trusting too much. I shall bear it. He cast aspersions on my mother. But I said nothing at first until he attacked me."

"What did he say about . . . hold it, I know. He said you were all Third World brothers, right?"

Chiun nodded.

"And when he said this he put his arm around you in a sign of friendship, right? And it was then that you cracked his wrist. Right?"

"I did not kill him, because I know your fear of notoriety. But there are no thanks for that. There are no thanks for his believing that he just cracked his wrist against a chair. There are no thanks for my deep concern for you and your organization to whom I have shown infinite loyalty. No. There are only monstrous threats against my most valued personal property."

"Yeah, well," said Remo, folding the green kimono on top of the other clothes in the huge suitcase, then snapping shut the lid, "you're coming with me. I wouldn't leave you alone here."

Remo would have sent Chiun back to Folcroft, but Folcroft was compromised by now. That was his first problem. His second was wondering how Chiun would act when they got to Human Awareness Laboratories.

He could not ask. Chiun had never taken kindly to prying into his life, let alone his emotions.

The receptionist counselor at the Human Awareness Laboratories assured Mr. Remo Donaldson and his physical education instructor that there was a very substantial reason why the two men could not register. HAL was booked for the next three years. Solid. But if Mr. Donaldson wanted to meet her after working hours and discuss possible enrollment in other similar awareness institutes, she would be happy to discuss it with him.

"More than happy, Mr. Donaldson." She was just shy of twenty and her thin white blouse barely disguised her hardening breasts. She ran her tongue over her clean young lips, letting her eyes drop below Remo's belt.

Remo leaned forward, where he could smell her subtle perfume. Her sleek brown hair hanging down to the nape of her neck brushed gently against Remo's lips at her ears, as he whispered very low in a voice that caressed her skin: "Look. You can register me. C'mon."

Simple words, slow and deep. Remo watched her face flush and felt her longing.

"I wish I could," she said weakly. "But Dr. Forrester registers all new participants. Oh, I wish, I wish I could."

"Get me Dr. Forrester. I'll speak to him."

"Her."

"Fine."

"If you see her, you won't want me."

"I'll always want you."

"Really?"

"No," said Remo and he leaned back and smiled at the vibrant young morsel.

"You're a bastard. A male chauvinist pig," she said.

"Yeah," said Remo. "A male chauvinist pig who's going to drive you up a wall."

"I'll phone but it won't do any good."

"Phone," said Remo, glancing around the spacious office. Everything about Human Awareness Laboratories was spacious, designed to be spacious, from the large plants in waist-high pots, to the roaringly large windows that opened the eyes to the sky and the earth and the trees in between. The young woman, her face still flushed with the excitement of the closeness of Remo, dialed the flat white phone at her glass-topped desk.

Remo strolled back to Chiun.

Chiun was absorbing the atmosphere, contemplating the openness of Human Awareness Laboratories. Without looking at Remo, he said: "You *are* a male chauvinist pig. I've never seen a more inept approach."

"I got what I wanted."

"Why didn't you threaten her with a gun? That would also have convinced her to call."

Remo picked up a brochure from a low, polished-steel table. He glanced at it and chuckled. "You're going to have to take your clothes off in front of people. Read this, Chiun."

Chiun ignored the brochure. "I will come to all problems with their solutions," he said, staring out the window, absorbing space.

Remo shrugged. He had never seen Chiun out of robes or uniforms. When Chiun bathed, he would sponge himself beneath the flowing robes of his daily garb. When he changed robes, he did so with such precision that one robe was going on as the other was coming off. Remo could never duplicate it — to some degree because he had never wanted to.

Dr. Lithia Forrester was in consultation when her phone rang. She ignored it because she was sure the switchboard would shut it off after the first accidental ring. She ignored it through five rings and then, realizing it was not accidental, she answered it.

"I told you I am never to be disturbed during consultations. We are fully registered for three . . . Donaldson? Remo Donaldson? Well, yes, I'll interview him. Send him up in fifteen minutes."

She returned the phone to the receiver with a surprisingly quivering hand and emitted a long, glorious shriek: "He's here. He's here. He's here."

"Who is here?" asked the person she was with.

"Someone I was trying to figure out how to get here. The one man who could spoil the plan. And now he's here. Talk of good fortune."

"Every silver lining has a cloud," said the person Dr. Forrester was with. But Lithia Forrester was hardly listening.

Before Remo Donaldson was allowed to enter, she reviewed the case alone.

Only an hour before, when he had failed to report, she had conceded Bannon's death. Careful, thorough, neat, orderly FBI Supervisor Bannon, who had managed to send so many government people to her. Probably dead. And his men too.

General Vance Withers. Dead.

The Special Forces colonel, a professional group assassin, dead. And his men.

So now, Remo Donaldson, thought Lithia Forrester, welcome to my lair. Welcome to the game of the mind where your brain and your testicles work against your survival. I know what you are now. You are a human weapon. You are going to meet a target that will consume you. She had been afraid when she had first thought of Bannon dead, but she was afraid no longer.

Dr. Forrester could not know that, many stories below, an aged Oriental, basking in the sun pouring through a large window, was thinking also. And what he was thinking was this:

"I have trained you well, my son, Shiva, Destroyer of Worlds. Go without fear into this trap of the mind. For as great as the danger, no danger has yet stopped the force of man. Neither the flood, nor the storm, nor the sea. And now, from your people, neither the space to the stars. Go now, the spirit of the Destroyer's mind rises above the petty schemings of other mortals."

And to the receptionist counselor who had told Mr. Donaldson, "You can go upstairs now, and don't forget about tonight," the aged Oriental appeared to be a cute, frail sort of thing. She leaned toward him and said, "Pardon me, sir, I don't mean to be nosey, but how do you get your nails so long?"

She smiled sweetly, the kind of smile that got her a car from her father when she was sixteen.

The sweet old man smiled back.

"You are being nosey."

Upstairs, Remo Williams, alias Remo Donaldson, entered a double door and saw the most beautiful woman he had ever stood near, not like a creation of nature but of the dreams of man.

She stepped forward to meet him. "Hello, Remo Donaldson. I've been waiting for you."

Thirteen

Human Awareness Laboratories was "a workshop of human motivation, an in-depth exploration and re-functioning of the coping mechanism through relevant action experiences."

That was what the brochure said.

To Chiun, as he told Remo while they unpacked in the room they shared, it seemed like a lot of people getting undressed, saying impolite things to each other, and then touching.

"Touching is part of it," said Remo. "Let me know if you see anything."

"What are you looking for?"

"I don't know."

"It must be thrilling to think like a white man. It is impossible to find what you do not seek, my son."

"So I'm your son again?"

"I do not hold grudges."

Chiun was pleased about something. Perhaps it had been the tests they had taken that afternoon. Remo had met Dr. Forrester — in his mind, she was Lithia now — and, because he had been overwhelmed with her beauty, had been able to do no more than give her his pat, phony little biography. She had scheduled him for immediate testing, and then dismissed him like a schoolmarm.

Even though he was not technically a participant, Chiun had taken the battery of psychological tests with Remo. Chiun had thought they were great good fun.

"Listen to this," he cackled. "What would you rather be: a cleaner of fish, a soldier, a garbage collector, an artist? Check one."

"So? Check one," Remo had said.

"I do not wish to be a cleaner of fish, a soldier, a garbage collector, or an artist. I check none," Chiun had said, and then defiantly had written across the paper, "I choose to be the Master of Sinanju."

If he had thought that test was funny, Chiun thought the test where they tried to form a batch of small blocks into a large cube was hilarious. Chiun had quickly formed a cube, but one block was left over. With the side of his hand, he had crushed the errant block into powder, and then sprinkled the dust over the large cube. "Done," he shouted triumphantly.

And so it had gone.

Remo did the best he could, and had no idea whether he had failed or passed. Assuming, of course, that one could fail or pass.

Just then, the phone in their small room rang. Remo picked it up. "Donaldson here," he said. A cold female voice told him that Dr. Forrester would see him. Immediately.

It was well into evening when Remo entered Lithia Forrester's office for the second time. She was standing against her desk, her back to him, and as Remo saw her, despite all his controls, he felt a deep longing for her, a longing beyond sex. It was a longing to reproduce with her.

"Sit down, Mr. Donaldson," she said, pointing easily to the couch. She picked up a sheaf of papers and walked to the couch and sat next to him. "I wanted to explain your test scores to you."

The blocks they had put together indicated perception and organization. High superior, Remo had gotten, which was a bit surprising because when he was Remo Williams and applying for the Newark, New Jersey, police department he had gotten average. Chiun was right. The muscles of the mind could grow, just as the muscles of the arms or legs.

Then came frustration elements. Remo's was high. A blotch of something or other showed that. "Your health instructor, however, scored very low," the lowest Dr. Forrester had ever seen. She leaned into Remo on the couch. "Why do you suppose his frustration level is so low?" she asked.

Her body was a perfume of rare elegance. "Because," Remo said, "he manages to diffuse frustration onto others."

"And here's something extraordinary. Both of you have nonexistent aggression quotients. I mean, they don't exist. That is impossible. Did you make up answers for the test?"

"Was that the one with the lines and arrows and things?" Remo asked.

"Yes."

"You got me," Remo said. He was interested. The test had seemed so harmless that both he and Chiun had answered honestly. "I don't know how you could make up answers to that test."

"That's how it was designed. Remarkable. Absolutely no trace of normal aggressive instincts." Lithia rose from the couch in a swirl of clinging jersey. "Make yourself comfortable," she said. "We must talk."

Remo leaned back into the leather couch and looked up at the darkening sky above the dome. A hawk pivoted far off, slowly — as if not moving, then suddenly diving. Remo could not see the target but he was sure the target was there. He was also sure that Lithia Forrester attacked like that. Why was it that most women and some men used sex as a weapon? Funny, that he should think about that now.

The woman sat in a leather chair facing him and began asking questions in her best Doctor Forrester tone.

"If someone got ahead of you on a long line to a movie, what would you do?"

"I'd point out to him that everyone had formed a line and he should recognize it."

"And if he refused?"

"So? What's one man? Frankly, I might not even point it out to him."

"Have you ever killed a man?"

"Oh sure. More than I remember."

"In Vietnam?"

"There too."

"What if I should tell you that we've checked on your records, Mr. Donaldson, and we find nothing. Nothing. You may know that these laboratories often deal with government personnel. Consequently, every participant is carefully screened. There seems to be no trace of you. Not even fingerprints."

"Well, I'll be."

"Mr. Donaldson, you came here and listed yourself as a professional golfer. There is no professional golfer named Remo Donaldson. You say you were in Vietnam but there are no military records of your existence. Mr. Donaldson. Just who are you?"

Remo smiled. It was time to join the issue and find out just who Dr. Forrester was. "I'm the man who's going to kill you." He watched her eyes and hands. No giveaway. Just another calm question. Perhaps that was the biggest giveaway there could be.

"Ah, aggression. Showing for the first time. Good. I think your problem is a fear of your aggression. An inability to accept your deep and raging hostility. Why do you want to kill me?"

"Who said I *wanted* to kill you? I'm going to kill you."

"You mean you don't want to kill me?"

"Not now. Not yet. Frankly, I think killing you would be like painting the *Pietà* pink. But I'll have to kill you."

"Why?"

"Because you probably should be killed."

"Why?"

"You're a hit."

"I see. Who decides who is a hit and who isn't?"

"By and large, me."

"How do you feel about your hits?"

"How do you feel about your patients?"

"I don't hate my patients."

"I rarely hate my hits."

"How many people have you killed, Mr. Donaldson?"

"How many people have you slept with?"

"Then it is a sexual thing with you?"

"No."

"What do you feel then when you kill someone?"

"A professional interest in the competence of my craft. I wonder afterwards if my left arm was straight."

"No emotion."

"Of course not. I'm the killer, not the killee." Remo laughed at his own little joke. He was not joined in the mirth, and his laughter died suddenly.

"No emotion," repeated Lithia Forrester. "Why do you kill people?"

"It's my job. Actually, my profession. I'm very good at it, Dr. Forrester. You might say it's a calling."

"How is your sex life?" she said, changing the subject.

"Adequate."

"How do you feel about your parents?"

74

"I don't know my parents. I was raised in an orphanage and I didn't feel all that much for the nuns who ran it. They were all right. They did the best they could."

"I see. Then you have no recollection of a male image. Describe to me the perfect man. Lie back if you wish, close your eyes, and if you can create the ideal man, create him for me."

Remo nodded and eased comfortably down into the couch. He kicked off his loafers.

"The ideal man," Remo said, "has a calm within him, a peace that is linked to the forces of the world. The ideal man seeks no unnecessary danger but accepts whatever danger there is, knowing that death is a natural part of life, knowing that it is how he dies, not when, that matters. I see the ideal man capable of sitting quietly for hours, his long, thin hands resting at peace upon his robes. I see the ideal man in command of his craft and doing what he must do as well as man can do it. I see the ideal man as a teacher of someone he loves."

Dr. Forrester's voice interrupted. "Is the Oriental your father?"

"No."

"Did he raise you, I mean?"

"Not as a child."

"Do you love him?"

Remo bolted upright on the couch. "None of your damned business."

"Well, for the first time we see aggressive emotion. There was almost no emotion as you spun the fantasies about killing people. What we're going to try to do, Remo, is in effect to assassinate the killer in you. That other you, that strong male image you never had as a child. We're going to help you form a new self-image, a positive force. And in your therapy, we will destroy that hostile fantasy. Do you have a name for him? Many people often do."

"Yes. The Destroyer."

"Good. Then we're going to have to kill the Destroyer. Together." She paused. "I'm afraid we're going to have to end this now. Time is up."

Remo stood, straight and balanced. He looked into the vibrant blue crystals of her eyes. Her calm smile both aroused and angered him. He smiled.

"Many have plotted the death of the Destroyer and together with their schemes have been stuffed into dirt."

"Well," Dr. Forrester said, smiling sweetly, "we'll see what we can do here at Human Awareness Laboratories."

And that was when Remo again felt the longing beyond the mere desire to penetrate. He wanted to reproduce.

So be it. Then this was where he might die. Remo gazed up again through the dome, searched the night sky with his eyes for the hawk. But the hawk was not there.

Fourteen

After Remo had left, Lithia Forrester sat down at her desk for long minutes, thinking.

Then she dialed three short digits on the telephone, calling one of the rooms at the Human Awareness Laboratories.

"Yes," answered a bored voice.

"He's just left," she said. "There's no doubt. He's been sent here to stop our plan."

"Then kill him," came the voice.

"Yes, of course. But I don't want to do it here. Too much attention brought to bear might spoil our plan."

"Well, do it anywhere you want. Just do it."

"Yes, yes, of course," Lithia Forrester said. Then she added softly, "Could I come down later? It's been so long."

"Not tonight. I'm tired."

"Please?" she said. "Please?"

There was a pause on the other end of the line, then a sigh. "Well, all right. If you really want to."

Lithia Forrester's golden face sparkled into a warm glow. "Oh, thank you," she said.

"Yeah, sure. As long as you're coming, bring some potato chips and dip. Onion dip. And a big bag of chips."

"I will. I will," she said happily and long after the abrupt click had died in her ear, she held the phone warmly to her breast, like a schoolgirl with a love letter.

Fifteen

It was morning and Chiun and Remo had to attend their first encounter session.

"Don't be nervous, Chiun. I want your promise that you won't let the words bother you. No matter what anyone says. It's just words."

Chiun glanced disdainfully at Remo, then back out at the rolling hills, as if words could never upset him.

Then they both left their room on the carpeted sixth floor where the sleep environments, as they were called, lined a central area called the mobile physical transition area — the hallway — to the elevators. Remo wondered what the elevators were called and was told by the elevator operator, "elevators."

"I thought it'd be something like bi-directional transition cells."

The elevator doors opened to a spacious room on the third floor. This was the major encounter room, carpeted on all four walls and the ceiling with a gray woolly material. Long, slit openings rent the gray carpeting to allow fluorescent lights to shine down. Giant pillows formed a circle in the center of the room. Ashtrays of pottery were at each pillow. The group was in progress as Remo and Chiun entered. Dr. Lithia Forrester sat on one of the pillows.

She was not talking. Immediately a balloon of a woman with a complexion of ravaged oatmeal and a tiny baby mouth that spewed venom demanded to know who Remo and Chiun were and why they felt they could walk in late. She said she resented Remo and Chiun, but Remo more than Chiun.

"Why do you resent Mr. Donaldson more than Mr. Chiun?"

"Because he walks in like he thinks I want him in me. He walks like King Shit. Well, he's not. I wouldn't let him touch me," she yelled, clutching her bulbous breasts in her pudgy hands. Stringy, sometimes blond, hair surrounded the oatmeal face like desecrated wheat. She wore shorts, her belly looked like a rubber inner-tube after a high compression pump had run amok. Her name was Florissa. She was a computer specialist at the Pentagon.

"How do you feel about that, Remo?" Dr. Forrester asked.

Remo shrugged and sat down. "Am I supposed to feel something?"

"I hate you," said Florissa. "I hate your maleness. You think you're so handsome everyone wants you."

"What do you feel, Remo?" asked Dr. Forrester.

"I think this is silly."

Florissa began to cry, as though her heavy mascara crop needed watering. Her face now looked as if it should be condemned by the health department.

Florissa said she felt rejected. The other members of the group, except Dr. Forrester and someone else, went to her, put their hands on her back and face, and began patting. They intoned that she was wanted and should not feel rejected. They told her she was loved. She had done beautifully. She had given of herself. She had given the entire group a beautiful moment.

"He doesn't think so," said Florissa. "He thinks I'm ugly. He doesn't want me."

Remo glanced briefly at the other member of the group who had not joined in the group consolation of Florissa. He was a huge man, not in height but in girth, weighing perhaps 450 pounds. He was as black as the last midnight of the world but his face, although enpuffed by billowing fat, remained strong. He reminded Remo of a great black king. He was so encumbered by weight he breathed heavily just to sit upright. As Remo watched, he kept spraying something into his mouth with a little rubber ball and a plastic tube device. It was for asthma. His black eyes burned as they looked over the apparatus at Remo. Formidable, Remo thought. Formidable.

Remo looked for Chiun, worried about what he might do. And then Remo blinked. Chiun had joined the group, and he was massaging Florissa's back. He motioned the other members away, then, working his delicate hands up and down her spine, he intoned: "You are the flower of all men's longing. You are graciousness flowing softly like the murmur of love from man to woman and from woman to man.

You are splendor of your kind, a jewel of rare and exquisite elegance. You are beautiful. You are woman."

Remo saw Tubbo lift her mascara-smeared puss. She was beaming. "I feel loved," she said.

"You are loved because you are loveable," said Chiun, "a precious loved flower."

"Make him love me."

"Who?"

"Remo."

"I cannot account for his ignorance."

Remo looked at Lithia Forrester and then realized the secret of group therapy. Those leading it had to keep a straight face. Then again, maybe it was good. Hadn't Chiun forced Remo in his training to examine his emotions, then use those that were beneficial?

Chiun returned in his little paddling walk to the open pillow near Remo. He sat down as he normally did, with a lightning-fast soft motion that looked slow, almost as if a feather were drifting to rest upon the pillow. Only after years of training could Remo duplicate the motion. Remo checked the faces to see who would recognize such body control. Again, his eyes rested on the black man's face. He was watching Chiun intently. Lithia Forrester had noticed nothing.

The group was told to identify itself; to say how each one felt about the newcomers, to guess what they did for a living.

A man in his mid-forties, who said he was not permitted to identify exactly what he did, said he felt rejected by the world and his society. He said he assumed both Remo and Chiun had government jobs because only cleared people could attend Human Awareness Laboratories.

"Remo is a health instructor in some military kind of thing and Chiun must be a translator of some sort for the state department's Japan desk."

Chiun answered. "You think I am Japanese. Therefore you work for the CIA. Correct? And you speak like a white man who has attempted for many years to master Mandarin. Correct? Therefore you work in the Asia section. Correct?"

"Amazing," said the man.

"You have just proven Communism is a failure," Chiun said. "To not succeed against you schmucks is the proof of Communism's failure. I am not Japanese."

80

"Chinese?" asked the CIA man.

"Schmuck," said Chiun, again using the word he had picked up from a Jewish woman at a Puerto Rican hotel. Chiun loved the word.

The CIA man lowered his head and then told the story of his career, how he had been an expert in grain production, one of the best, really he was. He was really good. He was so good he was promoted to the hot Asia section and put as second-in-command of operations. He had done so poorly in that job, he was left there.

"Typical," said the black man. "Typical." He did not want to identify himself or tell what he thought or felt.

Dr. Forrester prodded. She prodded while looking at Remo. Finally, the large black man told a story that left them all looking down at the carpet, not wanting to lift their heads.

Larry Garrand was born in Middle River, Connecticut. He wasn't fat then. Larry Garrand was a Boy Scout. Larry Garrand was president of his elementary school class. Larry Garrand was captain of the elementary school football team. Captain of the baseball team. Larry Garrand had the highest grades in his elementary school class. Yeah, some kids started skin-popping. A couple of the girls got pregnant at eleven years old. But they were the niggers. Larry Garrand and his family were different. They were the class. Not class because they were light. He never went for that. His family was class because his father was a high school teacher in Booker T. Washington High School, and he was black.

Larry didn't go to Booker T. He went to the white high school, James Madison. Oh sure, he knew there were racists there but that was because they didn't know substantial Negroes. They hadn't met good Negroes. Larry was going to show them. This white high school, James Madison High, was something else. Sure everyone thought Larry would make a great halfback.

"Halfback?" interrupted Remo.

Halfback, continued Larry Garrand. He smiled.

He was thin then and fast. Real fast. But he didn't want to make it running. He wanted to make it another way. He wanted to show the white folks that Negroes could cut the mustard in every way. Decent Negroes.

It was a whole new scene at Madison. First of all, his freshman year saw him in the lower third of his class. He had been first in elementary school. He knew what the whites were thinking. His father saw the report card and didn't say a word. What his father was really saying was that they weren't as good as whites, so why try? Larry Garrand tried. He read his lessons twice. He pretended, in front of the whites, that he didn't work hard. But he studied ten hours a day. During midterm recesses, he would begin reading for the next semester. Larry Garrand invented his own speed-reading.

It was the time of Malcolm X and Martin Luther King. Larry Garrand thought they were both wrong. When the whites saw how really top-notch Negroes could be, they would change their minds and not one second sooner. Larry Garrand won a scholarship to Harvard. He graduated magna cum laude despite severe headaches every two weeks. He went to many doctors, but none could cure him.

He had been approached by many white women but refused their offers. He wanted to show that black men — it had changed from Negro by then — weren't just interested in white pussy.

One night, the police made a dragnet pickup in Roxbury, the black section. They picked up Larry Garrand but when he showed who he was, they let him go. After all, he wasn't a nigger. Not all blacks were niggers, and whites were beginning to realize that.

When Afros first came out, Larry Garrand secretly died inside. They looked so stupid. So niggerish, if you want to know the truth.

Larry Garrand got a master's and then a doctorate, not in sociology or the other plush, easy courses that attracted most blacks. He got it in physics. The headaches got worse. But he had almost made it.

Dr. Lawrence Garrand went to work for the United States government's Atomic Energy Commission, and he was Dr. Garrand, and the secretaries called him "sir." He attended a cocktail party at the White House. In one discovery, he was noted in a national news magazine, his opinion sought by U.S. senators. Where he worked, it was Dr. Garrand this and Dr. Garrand that and Dr. Garrand will not be able to meet with you this week, Congressman, perhaps next.

When Dr. Garrand knew that he had become the world's foremost authority on atomic waste disposal, then he felt he could allow himself to indulge a secret boyhood wish. He bought himself a gold-colored Cadillac convertible. After all, for the foremost authority on atomic waste disposal, this was an eccentricity. Do you know that the foremost authority on atomic waste disposal drives a gold Cadillac?

He even indulged in a modified Afro, cut neat every week, of course. And well, since it was in, he bought a dashiki. The foremost authority on atomic waste disposal drives a gold Cadillac, wears an Afro and a dashiki. Dr. Garrand was the one really helping the Afro-American's cause, not the shouters.

One evening, while driving to New York City, not in Mobile or Biloxi or Little Rock, but in Jersey City, New Jersey, the world's foremost authority on atomic waste disposal was stopped by a motorcycle policeman. Not for speeding. Not for passing a red light or making an improper turn.

"Just for a check, buddy. Let me see your license and registration. Yeah, yeah, sure. You're the foremost authority on everything. You know it all."

"I was just trying to explain who I am."

"You're Mr. Wonderful. Keep your hands up on the wheel where I can see them."

"I'll have your badge, officer."

The motorcycle patrolman shined his flashlight directly into Dr. Garrand's eyes.

"I've had all I'm going to take from you. You shut up. Now open your hood."

Dr. Garrand pressed the hidden hood release, taking joy in his own anger, anticipating the glorious revenge when the patrolman was dressed down by his superior, who was dressed down from Washington.

Dr. Garrand heard noises as the policeman's head disappeared under the hood.

"Okay, follow me," said the patrolman, handing back the registration and license.

"Is there anything wrong?" asked Dr. Garrand.

"Just follow me. There will be a patrol car right behind us."

That night, the world's foremost authority on atomic waste disposal was booked at the Greenville Precinct, for incorrect registration of an auto. The motor mount number and the registration did not match. Dr. Garrand, if that was his name, was allowed one phone call. Since he did not know a politician other than the president and some senators, he called the head of the Atomic Energy Commission.

"Oh, I'm sorry, Larry, he isn't home. They're booking you for what?"

"Incorrect registration or something."

"That's incredible, Larry. Tell them to send you a letter. I'll tell him as soon as he gets home."

And that was Dr. Lawrence Garrand's phone call before he was placed in a cell block with a pimp who hadn't paid off, a drunk-and-disorderly, and a breaking-and-entering. All black.

He spent the night with the niggers, and just as red was coming into the gloomy cold gray, which he could see through the small, mesh-covered window, he realized something that made his headache go away.

There weren't three niggers and Dr. Lawrence Garrand in the cell. There were four niggers, one of whom claimed to be the world's foremost authority on atomic waste disposal.

And for some crazy reason, all he could think about was all the white pussy he had passed up.

The Atomic Energy Commission, of course, complained to the Jersey City cops. But Larry Garrand didn't care anymore. He was still called sir, still sought by senators, but Larry Garrand didn't care anymore. Because Dr. Lawrence Garrand, world's foremost authority on atomic waste disposal, knew that when push came to shove, when you're driving alone at night in Jersey City, you, Larry Garrand, are a nigger.

And that was the story. The room was silent.

Florissa pointed out that Dr. Garrand was allowing whites to define his terms of reference. The CIA man suggested emigration to Africa. Someone else suggested that overeating was no compensation, to which Dr. Lawrence Garrand answered that he had his own compensation, which was none of anyone's business. And Dr. Forrester did not push him to explain.

Then Chiun spoke.

"In the world, there are hundreds of flowers that bloom, each with its own beauty. Yet not one depends on the other's admission of it. Beauty is beauty, and one should accept the beauty that is his. For it is only his and no one else's."

Everyone thought that was a beautiful sentiment.

Remo whispered to Chiun: "Why don't you tell him about the clay that God burned too long? He'd love that one."

The group wanted to know what Remo was whispering and he advised one and all to blow it out their ears. This was considered hostile.

Florissa thought it was the most hostile, particularly now when she had almost forgiven Remo for not wanting to make love to her.

The class retired to womb-touching, floating-around in a pool nude, and leaning on people. Dr. Forrester was not present. Chiun sat fully robed on the pool's edge. He explained that to enter the pool nude was a violation of his cultural habits.

Remo tried the same thing. He was accused of having hang-ups. He explained that getting undressed in front of strangers was an American cultural thing too. It was decided loudly that American cultural things didn't count.

Remo stripped and climbed into the pool and everyone agreed that he managed to save the man who had gotten everyone to agree that American cultural things didn't count. It seemed Remo's hand accidentally slapped the man's face into the water and the man had trouble resurfacing. Then Remo helped him recover by special artificial respiration. "It only looks like I'm punching him in the stomach," Remo said.

Sixteen

The first sign that France would bid — yes, definitely bid — came when France began converting paper into gold in countries around the world.

First, it was South Africa from which France demanded, and got, $73 million in gold. And then France's top fiscal officer called the secretary of the treasury and told him that because of certain internal problems, France found it necessary to shore up the value of the franc with more gold. Well, the internal problems were of a secret nature and no, unfortunately, he could not speak about them, but the secretary of the treasury would understand. Yes, it was just a temporary thing. The secretary need not worry that France was making any effort to undermine the American dollar. The integrity of the franc was all that was being considered at this moment. He could not say any more, which was true for a very good reason: he did not know any more. All he knew were his instructions to begin accumulating more gold.

And soon, two hundred million more in gold was on its way to France's national bank.

The secretary of the treasury was perplexed. Ordinarily, governments conduct business much as bookies do with habitual gamblers — by telephone and pieces of paper and record-keeping — but only rarely by actual exchanges of money. Yet, in the emerging world, France was an ally and allies must be kept happy.

The signs of what France was doing were immediately evident to Mr. Amadeus Rentzel of the House of Rapfenberg, but he was still not happy. On the international scene, France was a putz, epitomized by de Gaulle's anguished question: "How can one govern a country that produces 117 different kinds of cheese?" On the mind of Mr. Amadeus

Rentzel were Great Britain and Russia, which had not yet indicated any real interest in bidding.

It simply would not do to have even one country fail to bid after having been invited, because that country might just alert the United States to what was happening — and that could be disastrous to their plan.

That day, Rentzel began to make discreet inquiries. The answers were quick in coming. England and Russia might indeed be interested in bidding. Yes, the nuclear bomber thing was interesting. So were the revelations by the CIA man. But, after all, they were really in the nature of parlor tricks. What about sea power? What kind of guarantee was there that the package would include control of the U.S. Navy operations? True to its history and its habits, Great Britain looked for control of U.S. Navy strength. And true to its history of seeking sea power and sea ports, Russia wanted to know the same things.

That night, Mr. Amadeus Rentzel, Swiss banker, spoke long distance to a private telephone in the United States.

"John Bull and Ivan are the only holdouts. They won't bid until we show them something involving the Navy."

The bored, languid voice answered: "How much do they expect us to show. We've gone through the Air Force and the CIA already."

"I know," Rentzel said. "I've explained that. But they won't budge."

There was a pause, then the long sigh of a person much used to being put upon by the world. "All right. We'll try to do something quickly. The other countries are in line?"

"Yessir. Literally itching to go ahead. I'm sure you've noticed the money movements in the financial pages?"

"Yes, yes, of course. All right. We'll give them something with the Navy."

Dr. Lithia Forrester sat in her domed tenth-floor office at the Human Awareness Laboratories pondering a difficult question. Remo Donaldson must go. But how?

The end button on her telephone began to blink on and off, splashing a spray of light onto the darkened desk. She picked up the telephone rapidly.

"Yes?"

"Do something with the Navy."

"Such as?"

"Such as anything you want, bitch. Just do it big and do it fast. It's important."

"Yes, dear, of course." She paused. "Will I see you tonight?"

"I think we might be doing better on our plans if you thought less about sex and more about our project."

"That's not fair," she said. "I've done everything I could do. Everything you wanted me to."

"Then let your sense of accomplishment serve as your sexual gratification. Just get started. Do something with the Navy."

The phone clicked off in Lithia Forrester's ear. She slowly replaced the receiver on the stand. Then she leaned back in her glove-leather chair and looked up at the dome, out at the night sky, the free night sky of America . . . the sky which, if they had their way, would not be free much longer.

Only three more days, she thought, until the bidding was held. It must be important to be required on such short notice.

Something with the Navy. Something big and fast. But what?

And what of her other problem? Remo Donaldson.

Perhaps something to take care of two birds with one stone?

Seventeen

Dr. Lithia Forrester did not attend the next morning's encounter session.

And while Remo Williams sat there, enduring the baleful looks of the black behemoth, Dr. Lawrence Garrand, and tried to tune out his ears to the verbal assaults dictated by Florissa's sexual insecurity, he made a decision.

Chiun and he had been at the Human Awareness Laboratories for thirty-six hours and nothing had happened. Remo had laid it out to Lithia Forrester in that first interview, telling her he was going to kill her, inviting her to move against him. But she had done nothing and he could wait no longer. This day, he would get to Lithia Forrester, and he would break her. And if need be, he would kill her.

That prospect disquieted him. He told himself he was only being professional. There was too much he did not know about the scheme; too many things to find out first. He could not kill her until he found out.

But the picture of Lithia Forrester kept edging into his mind, the tall, elegant, beautiful blondness of her. And he realized his decision not to kill her had nothing to do with being professional.

All right, he would kill her. But first, he would make love to her.

As a professional, Remo feared, he was a zero. He had found out nothing, had seen nothing suspicious. He had not learned anything that would tie in to Bannon or to the Special Forces colonel or to the pilot that bombed St. Louis or to the CIA man, Barrett.

He felt a discontent rising in him — not at himself for ineptitude, but at Smith for sending him here on a detective's mission. If they needed information, why not send Gray, that new guy at the FBI, or

Henry Kissinger, or even hire Jack Anderson? Why Remo? It didn't matter; the others might be already compromised.

Remo was deep in his thoughts when he felt the movement of the group and realized they were rising from their cushions, the session over. Then they headed to the door, Chiun leading the group, gesticulating with his hands on the need to bury one's aggressions and to learn to accept the world for what it was.

The group jammed into the hall doorway, Remo slowly trailing behind, still thinking. And then he heard it again. That song. Someone in the group was humming, and he realized it was that song that Bannon had hummed, the same one that had been hummed in Remo's face by the colonel he had killed on the golf course. Remo snapped to full alertness; his eyes searched the encounter group's members, looking for the musician.

But then the sound stopped, and as hard as Remo looked, he could find no trace of whom it had come from.

Lithia Forrester had missed the encounter session that morning because she was not at the Human Awareness Laboratories. She was in a Washington hotel room, explaining something very important to Admiral James Benton Crust.

Admiral Crust had not forgotten the woman he had met several nights before at the party in the French ambassador's home. If the truth be told, he had thought of little else but her in the four days since, for a strange stirring that he had not felt for years had awakened his loins.

So, when she had phoned him that morning in his office at the Pentagon, he had, of course, remembered her. And he had been only too happy to meet her, any place she suggested, and when she suggested a room in an out-of-the-way hotel because of "the nature" of their meeting, he had agreed very formally and then, after hanging up the telephone, had done a very uncharacteristic war whoop in his office.

On the way to the hotel, Admiral Crust did another uncharacteristic thing. He had his chauffeur stop at a liquor store and buy a fifth of bourbon — the best bourbon — and he felt somehow wicked and schoolboyish as he carefully placed the bottle into his large leather attaché case.

When the admiral entered the hotel room, Lithia Forrester was already there. She stood at the window, looking out over the busy noontime streets of Washington, D.C. She wore a thin silk paisley dress; the daylight pouring through the window silhouetted her body under the clothes as if she were naked. Crust could see she wore no undergarments; when she turned to greet him, her breasts bobbed under the thin fabric, and he again felt that tinge that, for years, he had thought he was beyond feeling.

The sunlight pouring into the room competed with her smile for the honor of lighting up the room. The sunlight lost. She smiled with her mouth, with her eyes, and with her body, and she came forward to greet him with her arms extended.

"Jim, I'm so glad you're all right," she said.

Suddenly, Admiral Crust felt foolish at the thought of the bottle of bourbon in the attaché case and he set it down beside the door. For a moment, he was afraid to meet her eyes, lest she read in his what he had been thinking about in the car on the way over. Then he said gruffly, "Lithia. How are you, my dear?"

She took his elbows in her hands, kissed him on the cheek, then took his hand and led him to the sofa, steering him gently to sit on it. She pulled a fabric-covered chair over close to the couch and sat facing him across a Formica-topped coffee table.

"Jim, I know how busy you must be and I'm sorry to disturb you." He waved away any idea of disturbance and he noticed how the sunlight still shone through her dress as she changed position in the chair and how golden her hair was in the clear rays coming into the room. She smelled of rare jasmine. She went on, "but I think your life's in danger."

Admiral James Benton Crust laughed. "My life in danger? From whom? Or from what?"

"From whom," she said. "From one of my patients. A Remo Donaldson. He's threatened to kill you."

"Remo Donaldson? I've never heard of him. Why should he want to kill me?"

"I don't know. That's what terrifies me," she said. As she slid forward in her seat, her dress rode up above her knees and the golden hairs on her thighs glinted yellow and white in the sunlight. "But I think he's in the employ of an enemy power."

Crust smiled, as if to dismiss any threat to his person that could come from a Remo Donaldson, but Lithia Forrester went on quickly: "Jim, this is no laughing matter. Do you realize that I've violated a sacred doctor-patient relationship to come here and tell you this?"

She rose from her chair and walked around to sit down beside him on the couch. Through the shiny blue gabardine of his uniform trousers, he could feel the warmth and pressure of her thigh, raising the hairs on his leg.

"I appreciate that, Lithia. Suppose you tell me about it from the beginning."

"He came to me only a few days ago. He lied to me on his admissions form but — frankly — that's not unusual. We have so many government personnel, and they often use false identities to join our groups. But under hypnosis last night, I succeeded in breaking through this Remo Donaldson." She looked into the admiral's face. She was, he thought, only a kiss away. "Jim, he's a professional assassin. And his next target is you — Admiral Crust. He told me."

"Did he say why? Why me?" Crust asked.

"No. And he was slipping back to the conscious level, so I couldn't press him. So, I don't know why, I don't know where, and I don't know when. But I do know, Jim, he plans to kill you."

"Well, there's one sure way to deal with this," Crust said. "Call the FBI. Have him picked up. Find out just what the hell's on his mind."

He began to get to his feet, but Lithia caught his arm and pulled him back down to her. She turned on the sofa slightly so she was facing him, but all he realized was that his left knee was pressed between both her knees.

"You can't do that, Jim," she said. "He's a professional. I don't think picking him up would accomplish anything, and besides, it would compromise me and my work. The thing to do is to let me keep working on him. But in the meantime, you must take steps to guard your own safety."

"Do you think you'll be able to find out what he's after?" Crust asked.

"We have another session tonight. With luck, I'll know then what his plan is." She smiled. "I'm really very good about getting information. Especially from men."

"I'll bet you are," Crust said, smiling back.

92

"Particularly men with problems. The kind of problems I can solve."

She smiled at him again and her eyes melted into his. They were the bluest eyes he had ever seen, a brilliant, piercing blue, the kind of blue generally reserved for a child's glass marble. Softly, she placed a hand on his knee. He could smell her perfume now, the rich powerful jasmine that made his breathing alive again.

They talked more. It was agreed that Admiral James Benton Crust would, that day, sign orders assigning himself as captain of the battleship *Alabama* that lay at anchor in Chesapeake Bay. His rank and position as chief of operations allowed him to do that. And he would move aboard the ship for the next few days, and he would assign a crew of frogmen to serve as his personal bodyguards, with orders to intercept Remo Donaldson should he try to reach the admiral, using any force that might be necessary. Including deadly force.

Admiral Crust agreed to all this because it was impossible to refuse anything to the golden beauty who sat next to him on the sofa. But, frankly, he thought the precautions were foolish.

"I still don't understand why anyone would want to attack an empty old wreck like me."

"Oh, Jim. You're not empty, you're not old, and you're not a wreck. You're a vibrant, warm human being. It's my business to know," she said. "Just as it's my business to understand that you've got some kind of serious problem on your mind."

"Problem?" Crust waved away any problem, but when he turned his face back, her eyes were still searching into his and he knew those blue eyes knew just what his problem was.

"Why don't you rest a few minutes, Jim, and tell me about it? I'm really a good listener," Lithia Forrester said. She took his head in her hands and slowly pulled it down until he was resting in her lap. Admiral Crust stretched his legs out along the length of the couch and looked up at the ceiling, trying to avoid her eyes.

"It's really embarrassing," he said.

"I'm a doctor, Jim. I don't embarrass easily. And there aren't many things I haven't heard," she said, placing a hand alongside his head, a finger casually touching the center of his ear. He could feel the warmth of her body now through the thin silk, and his senses felt flooded with the womanly smell of her.

Finally, he blurted it out.

"I haven't been a man for five years."

"Why do you think that?"

"I'm impotent. Just worthless. When I talk about an empty wreck, I'm not joking. I am an empty wreck."

"Have you tried?" she asked.

"Yes. Or at least I used to. And then I stopped trying. I had no desire; not to fail again."

"Maybe it was the woman?"

"Women," he corrected. "And who it was didn't matter. It was the same with every one of them. I felt no desire. And I haven't felt any for five years . . . until . . ."

"Until?" she said, the tone of her voice teasing him.

He was silent for a moment. "Until I saw you at that party," he blurted out. Admiral Crust closed his eyes so he would not have to suffer the laughter on her face when he said, "Lithia, I think I'm in love with you."

His eyes were still closed as she leaned forward, her face almost touching his. Softly, she said, "I didn't hear you say *that* at the party, Jim. But I did overhear you say something else. If memory serves me right, what you said was 'a tit is a tit.'" His eyes were still closed tightly and then he heard the sound of a zipper slowly opening.

He could feel her breath on his face. "Isn't that what you said, Jim? A tit is a tit," she whispered.

He felt confused and apologetic. How could he tell her that all breasts were alike to the man who had no feeling for breasts? He opened his eyes to tell her that. She had unzipped her dress and slid it off her shoulders, baring her perfect, golden breasts to him. They hung over him, cantilevered over his face, and their hard points told a story all their own.

"Do you still believe that, Jim?" she asked, and beyond her breasts, he could see that vital, loving face smiling down at him. "Do you believe that? That all tits and all women are alike?"

Admiral James Benton Crust raised himself to a sitting position, and brought his lips heavily onto Lithia Forrester's. It wasn't just a vague remembered tingle he felt now. It was a roaring burst of growing passion, and she kissed him hotly but with tenderness, and reached her hand down to his trousers, then freed her mouth to say,

"Another medical miracle performed." She smiled and he crushed her smile again with his mouth.

For the first time in five years, Admiral James Benton Crust was a young man. He would have her. He would have this vibrant golden girl and the intensity of his ardor would make up for five lost years.

"Do you want me, Jim?" she asked huskily.

"I need you. I have to have you," he said.

"You will," she said and kissed him again, long and searchingly. Then she stood up, and her silken dress dropped around her ankles. Provocatively lush, richly naked, she walked across the room to a table where her own briefcase lay. She opened it and took out a bottle of brandy and two glasses, then turned and faced him, openly, without embarrassment.

"You will have me, Jim," she said. "But first we will have a drink. And then I want you to hum a little song with me."

Admiral James Benton Crust no longer felt guilty about the bottle of bourbon in his own attaché case.

Eighteen

Chiun was out gamboling in the fields with the members of their encounter group when Remo slipped from the main building of the Human Awareness Laboratories and went to find a telephone.

It was high noon, but it was after 1 P.M. when Remo had finished walking the 6.3 miles of rolling road on the laboratory's grounds and found himself out on the main highway in a public telephone booth.

He dialed the special no-toll number and it had not completed even one ring before it was picked up.

"Smith."

"Remo."

"Anything to report?"

"Not a damned thing. I did everything but mug the woman who runs the joint when I first got here. Then I sat back and waited. But nothing's happened."

"To keep you up to date," Smith said dryly, "it looks as if France will be in the bidding. We're trying to find out now when and where it will be held. There are other countries involved too. We can tell by the gold movements. But still nothing from Russia and England, as far as we can tell."

"Well, that doesn't mean anything to me," Remo said. "Listen, I'm going to tackle this Dr. Forrester head-on and see if she cracks. I'd just put her away, but I don't think I ought to do that until I find out how she does whatever it is she's planning to do."

"Stay with it," Smith said. "Use your own judgment, but remember how important it is."

"Yeah, yeah. Everything's important. By the way, you know anything about music?"

Smith paused a moment, then asked: "What kind of music?"

"I don't know. Music music. That FBI guy Bannon — I guess you read about him — he was humming some kind of song that seemed to turn him into a maniac. And that Special Forces colonel on the golf course, he was humming it too. And today, I heard it here. I think it's all the same song. Mean anything to you?"

"It might," Smith said. "How's the song go?"

"For Christ sake," Remo said. "I'm not Alice Cooper. How the hell do I know how it goes? Da da da da da dum da dum . . ."

"I think you've got it wrong," Smith said. "How about da da da da dum da dum dum da da da da dum dum?"

"By George, I think you've got it," Remo said. "Where'd you learn it?"

"General Dorfwill was humming it when he bombed St. Louis. Clovis Porter was whistling it before he decided to go swim in a stream of sewage. And we think the CIA man, Barrett, was humming it when he strangled himself in the library."

"So what's it mean?" Remo asked.

"I don't know. It might be some kind of recognition signal. Or something else. I don't know."

"You're a great help," Remo said. "You ever think of a show-business career? We could cut a demo of that song. Call ourselves the CURE. All. Chiun could play drums."

"Afraid not," Smith said. "I'm tone deaf."

"Since when has that had anything to do with making a record? You'll hear from me," Remo said, then added, "Be careful. They know about me, so they may know about you."

"I've taken precautions," Smith said, quietly surprised that Remo even cared.

"Okay," Remo said and hung up.

Remo felt flat and he decided to do exercise roadwork along the highway before returning to his room at the Human Awareness Laboratories. It was almost 3 P.M. before he found himself walking rapidly along the winding roads inside the gate, the ten-story main building rising in front of him. Remo heard a car coming along the road behind him, stopped and turned. Dr. Forrester's gray chauffeur-driven Rolls-Royce pulled alongside him and stopped.

The rear door on Remo's side opened and Lithia Forrester's voice called out: "Mr. Donaldson. Get in. I'll drive you up."

Remo slipped into the back seat, closed the door, and turned to look at Lithia as the heavy car began to move silently forward. Her golden-blond hair flowed loosely around her face and her silken dress was wrinkled.

"You look like you just crawled out of the sack," Remo said.

"You're very perceptive," Lithia Forrester said softly. "Any other observations?"

"Yeah. It wasn't very good."

"How can you tell?"

"By your eyes. They've still got dots of light in them. If it had been any good, those lights would be out."

"You sound like an expert on putting out lights."

"I am," Remo said.

"I must impose upon you for instructions," Dr. Forrester said.

"Pick a time," Remo said. "How about tonight? I've got nothing booked except a yell-in with the other looney-tunes in this place. Then we have our nude splash party from 8 to 9. Then we play grab-ass from 9 until 9:30 or until Florissa gets tired of chasing me, whichever comes first."

"Let's make it tonight," she said. "My office, after dinner. Say 7 o'clock."

"You've got a date," Remo said. He leaned toward her as the car rolled to a stop in front of the ten-story main building. "Keep a light on for me."

"You're the only one I'd let turn them out," she said as Remo slid from the car. The door closed behind him and the car rolled off to the rear of the building where the parking garage and Lithia Forrester's private elevator were located.

Remo decided to pass up supper in the lab's communal dining room, despite Chiun's insistence that the vegetables were excellent, grown organically, and would give him the strength he needed for whatever mission lay ahead.

"How about a dozen raw clams?" Remo said. When he saw Chiun's look of disgust, he said, "Skip it."

Lithia Forrester's secretary was no longer at her desk when Remo stepped from the elevator on the tenth floor. He approached the double oaken doors that marked the way to Lithia Forrester's office and apartment, and knocked.

"Come in," she called.

Remo pulled open one of the heavy doors and walked inside. The lighting inside the office was subdued and the gathering gloom of dusk from the overhead dome cast a dullish light over the office, the kind of evening light that could vanish in seconds. Lithia Forrester had changed into a red silk hostess gown. She held two snifters of brandy in her hands.

"Remo. I'm glad you came," she said and stepped up to him, extending one of the glasses. He took it without enthusiasm, then raised it to clink against hers.

"To turning off the lights," she said, burying her face deep in the glass as she sipped from it.

Remo raised the glass and let some of the liquid go into his mouth before carefully slipping it back into the glass. How long had it been since he had had a drink? The unaccustomed liquid burned his tongue and the inside of his mouth where it touched flesh, but it also kindled up memories of earlier days when Remo could drink a tubful if he wanted, and needed answer to no one but his head. That was another thing Chiun had ruined for him. Liquor. Just as he had ruined sex by making it a discipline. The last time Remo had enjoyed sex had been with that politician's daughter in New Jersey, and that had ended in death.

So now he made believe he sipped the brandy and he raised the glass to Lithia Forrester. "To turning off the lights," he repeated. Well, maybe just one wouldn't hurt. Get into the spirit of the evening. He looked over the rim of the glass at Lithia Forrester's long, lush body wrapped in the rippling folds of red silk, her breasts rising high and proud over the sash around her waist, and again he felt that desire that went beyond lust.

He raised the glass to his mouth, drained it all in one swallow. It burned going down, which was what good brandy should do, having been made to sip. But it had a different kind of burn to it, too, and Remo rolled the aftertaste around in his mouth before he realized the drink had been drugged. He remembered the lessons and lectures from his early days with CURE. There was no mistake.

His brandy had been drugged.

Instead of anger, Remo felt joy. He had been waiting for *it* — for something — to happen and now *it* was happening. They were coming. He would not have to beat it out of Lithia Forrester and he would not have to kill her . . . not just yet . . . not before he had made real love to her and had let her know what it meant to a woman to have the lights in her eyes go out.

Remo could feel the drug now entering his bloodstream. He smiled at Lithia again across the glass and then she put her glass down on the desk and took his arm. "Come. Sit with me on the sofa," she said. And Remo walked slowly with her, breathing deeply into his lungs, forcing his heartbeat higher, demanding that his heart flood his blood and the cells of his body with oxygen, hyperventilating to counteract the effects of the drug. Lithia Forrester led him to the leather sofa and put him down on it, then sat next to him. She took his empty glass from his hand and placed it on the floor, then took the hand and placed it on her thigh.

The oxygen coursing through his body heightened his tactile sensations and he could feel under his fingertips the individual fibers of the silk and under the silk, the soft, smooth, seemingly pore-free surface of her leg. She turned him around and pulled him down so that his head was in her lap. He lay down comfortably as if to rest, but the brief flurry of drowsiness had passed; the oxygen had done its work and Remo was again in full control of his mind and body, the drug converted by the body's chemistry and by Chiun's training into just another harmless substance. Remo allowed her to place his head just right in her lap, then he closed his eyes and pretended to drift off to sleep.

He began to pull air slowly into his lungs to slow the beat of his heart, to counteract the brief flash of dizziness that always follows hyperventilation. Then he was breathing deeply, soundly, to all appearances fast asleep, and Lithia Forrester opened the buttons of his shirt and ran a finger down along his chest, making gentle, just-touching circles with her fingertip and nail.

"You will listen to me and hear only my voice," she said.

Remo snorted slightly through his sleep.

"What is your name?"

"Remo . . . Donaldson," he said slowly.

"For whom do you work?"

"The CIA."

"Who is The Destroyer?"

"Me. Code name," he said, intentionally slurring the words as if talking through a mouthful of sleep.

"Why are you here?"

"Plot. Against America, Have to find out who."

"Do you know who is doing it? Who is behind the plot?"

"No," Remo said. "Don't know."

"Remo, listen to me carefully," she said. "I'm going to help you. Do you hear me? Help you."

"Hear you."

"There *is* a plot against our nation. A plan to take over the United States. One man is behind it. His name is Crust. Admiral James Benton Crust. Repeat that."

"Admiral Crust. James Benton Crust."

"Admiral Crust is an evil man," Lithia Forrester said. "He wants to take over the country. He must be stopped. You must stop him."

". . . must stop him."

"He is aboard the battleship *Alabama* in Chesapeake Bay. Within hours, he will begin his plan to conquer America. You must stop him. Do you know how?"

"Know how . . . no . . . don't know how."

"You will get aboard the *Alabama*. And you will kill Admiral Crust. Understand? Repeat it."

"Will kill Admiral Crust. Stop plan to conquer America," Remo said.

"You will do it tonight. Tonight, understand?"

"Understand . . . kill Crust tonight."

Her finger played softly with Remo's left nipple. She leaned forward and talked softly into his ear.

"Do you like sex, Remo?"

"Like sex. Yes."

"Would you like to have me?"

"Yes. Have you."

"You will sleep now," she said. "When you awake, you will feel refreshed. We have made love, Remo. You have shown me what real lovemaking is. You have put out the lights in my eyes. It felt good, Remo. I never had it feel so good. When you wake up, you will remember how good it was. And then you will kill Admiral Crust and save our country. Now you will sleep. Sleep, Remo. Sleep."

"Sleep. Must sleep," Remo said and again began to breathe the heavy breaths of a man on the verge of snoring.

Lithia Forrester slid out easily from under his head and gently placed his head down onto the sofa. Remo lay there, feigning sleep, his mind racing. She must want him to kill Crust. But why? Had Crust found out something? Was he refusing to follow orders? Or was Crust her boss and was she just trying to get him out of the way?

And then Lithia Forrester made a mistake — a mistake that told Remo that Crust was not her boss and guaranteed that Crust would not die at Remo's hands. She walked to her desk in the now-dark office and as Remo watched through a slit eyelid, she picked up the phone and dialed three digits.

"How was dinner?" she asked.

Pause. Must be somebody in the laboratories, Remo thought. The three digits meant an internal call.

"It's all taken care of," she said. "Just the way you wanted it." So there was someone else. She had a partner, or even more likely, a boss.

Pause.

"Tomorrow," she said. What was tomorrow? Maybe his killing of Crust was supposed to set something in motion?

She spoke again. "I love you." Then she hung up.

Lithia Forrester was happy. Tonight, the meddlesome Remo Donaldson would be killed by Admiral Crust and his bodyguards. And then, tomorrow, Crust would provide the naval incident that was needed to get England and Russia to bid. It was perfect, a foolproof plan. She looked up at the dome that covered her office and laughed aloud, a high, piercing laugh that shattered the stillness of the office. Then she began to hum, the melody Remo had heard so many times in the last few days, the melody that somehow seemed to trigger disaster and death.

And for the first time Remo recognized the tune.

Lithia Forrester stood up and walked back toward the sofa. She stood in front of Remo, looking down at him, then opened her robe and pulled it back, exposing her naked body. Then she leaned forward over Remo, pressing a breast against his bare chest.

"Remo," she whispered. "Wake up."

Slowly, Remo began to stir and then to move. And then he opened his eyes wide, looked up and saw Lithia's face just inches above him.

He reached up and pulled her down to him and kissed her heavily on the mouth.

"And that's what it's like," he said. He looked at her eyes. "Go look in the mirror. You'll see the lights are out."

"I know they are, Remo," she said. "It was never so good before."

Remo stood up.

"Will you stay? I want to do it again," she said.

"Can't," he said. "Have something to do. But remember, when you need a man, I'm around. I'll be glad to turn your lights out again anytime." He stepped up to her and slid his hands under her red robe and squeezed her behind, hard, pinching it enough to hurt.

Then Remo turned and left, to go warn Admiral James Benton Crust that his life was in danger.

Nineteen

A cruise ship at night, with its strings of lamps and its decks illuminated by floodlights, is an ocean-going prostitute. A Navy ship, on the other hand, is a working girl, poor but honest. No frills or frippery, designed for the long haul — for marriage, not a roll in the hay.

The battleship *Alabama* was that kind of ship, Remo thought, as he stood on the wave-slapped dockside and looked out into Chesapeake Bay and saw the ship at rest four hundred yards off-shore, glinting dull gray in the glare of an occasional light, a mountain of metal in a briny wash.

What he could not see at that distance were the dozen heavily armed men, wearing the patches of Underwater Demolition Teams, prowling the ship, on special assignment from Admiral Crust to guard his person, to shoot first and ask questions later.

Nor could Remo see Admiral Crust in the captain's quarters behind the control room, lying in a large plush bed that the Navy insisted on calling a bunk.

Admiral Crust's thoughts were not on any purported threat to his life, nor were his thoughts any more military than those of any young sailor in a strange port on a weekend pass. Admiral James Benton Crust was thinking about getting laid.

After five years, it was pleasant again just to think about it and to know that it was possible. Lithia Forrester had proved that to him that afternoon.

Lithia Forrester. It would have been romantic, he thought, to say that if he never saw her again, his life would be empty. Romantic but inaccurate. She had given him the means again to make his life full and rich. And like any other good gift, its utility did not depend upon the presence of the giver.

He was sure he loved her, but he was equally sure he could love another as well. He meant to put that theory to the test. To many tests, he thought with a chuckle.

Down below the admiral's cabin, sixty feet below, at the waterline, a small powerboat, its engine off, drifted quietly through the dark to the side of the ship, close in under the overhang where it could not be seen by anyone on deck. Remo Williams tied the boat to a heavy line trailing down from the bow of the ship. He leaped up from the seat of the small boat and caught the heavy line in his hands. Like an ape, he clambered up the water-slicked rope hand over hand. At the top, he caught a hand onto the railing of the deck and pulled himself up high enough to see through one of the cutouts in the steel hull of the ship.

A man wearing a light denim jacket over a T-shirt and denim pants walked along the deck near Remo, cradling a shotgun in his arms. At a glance, Remo could see two other men, both carrying weapons, farther along toward the stem of the ship. Guards.

Remo waited until the man at the bow walked slowly by him and had his back to Remo. Noiselessly, Remo hoisted himself up over the low deck wall and on silent feet raced the twenty yards to a door in the ship's side. He slid inside quickly and found himself in a narrow corridor. Remo took off his white sports shirt and turned it around so that the buttons were behind his neck. At a fast glance, it might look like a T-shirt, and with Remo's dark slacks, he might look enough like a sailor to avoid rousing suspicion.

Remo began to work his way up stairwells, heading for where he knew the captain's cabin would be. After three flights, the steps ended. He turned left into a passageway, then darted quickly back into the opening to the stairwell.

A sailor with a shotgun stood in front of a door in the center of the passageway. That must be the captain's cabin.

Remo thought for a moment, then took a tank-type fire extinguisher down from the wall next to him. Cradling it in his arms like a baby, he began to whistle and quickly stepped off into the passageway, his feet wide apart, affecting the seaman's rolling walk. Up ahead, the sailor sprang to attention as Remo drew near. Remo grinned, nodded at him, and kept walking.

"Hold it," the sailor called. "Where are you going?"

"Replacing that fire extinguisher down there," Remo said, holding the tank high in his arms to hide his shirt. "It's got to be recharged."

The man with the gun hesitated, then said, "All right. Step it up."

"Aye, aye," Remo said and then took a step forward, drawing abreast of the man. He spun and tapped him alongside the head with the heavy galvanized tank of the extinguisher. The man dropped heavily to the floor. He would be unconscious for quite a while, Remo thought.

Inside his cabin, Admiral Crust sat up on his bed. He was going to telephone Lithia Forrester. Maybe see her again tomorrow. If need be, even sign up for her stupid therapy program.

Crust's head snapped up as his cabin door flew open and a man slid in, closing the door rapidly behind him.

"Admiral Crust?" the man asked.

"Who'd you expect? John Paul Jones? You've got a hell of a nerve parading in here without knocking."

"Admiral, who I am isn't important. I've come to tell you your life's in danger."

Another nut come to warn him about Remo Donaldson, Crust thought. But then he looked into the hard eyes of the man facing him across the cabin and he knew that this was Remo Donaldson. Best to play it easy and gentle.

"Come in, man," the admiral said. "What's this all about?"

"Admiral, I believe you know a Dr. Lithia Forrester?"

"Yes, that's right."

"Well, she plans to kill you. In fact, she thinks I'm here right now killing you for her."

"I've only met this Forrester woman twice," Crust said. "Why would she want to kill me?"

"She's involved in some kind of scheme against our country, Admiral. I don't know all the details of it. But somehow you're in her way and she plans to kill you."

"And who are you? How do you know all this?"

"Just a government employee, Admiral," Remo said, stepping another pace into the room. "And it's my business to know."

"What would you recommend I do?"

"The guards are a good idea on the ship. Double them. And tell them no one is to be allowed access to you. At least for the next couple of days."

"Things will be safe in a couple of days?" Crust asked.

"Things will be over in a couple of days," Remo said. "Admiral, I don't have much time. But believe me. This is important. Stay out of sight. Stay away from Dr. Forrester. Be careful. I'm sorry that I can't tell you any more."

"Secret, hmmm?"

"Top secret, Admiral."

Behind Remo, the door flew open and he felt a gun barrel pressed against the base of his skull.

"Admiral. Are you all right?"

"Yes, Chief, I am. What happened to the man outside the door?"

"Knocked out. We saw him in the hall and decided to take a chance and bust right in."

"Good thing you did," the admiral said, still sitting on his bed. The phone at his elbow began to ring. He held up a hand to the three sailors behind Remo, indicating they should wait a moment, and lifted the phone to his ear.

"Yes, Lithia," he said. "Just a moment." He smiled at Remo. Deep down in his stomach Remo felt the tension of being trapped. "Men," Admiral Crust said, "I want you to take Mr. Remo Donaldson here back to shore. Make sure he has an interesting voyage," he said, smiling.

"We will, Admiral. Very interesting," said the sailor who held the gun at Remo's neck. "Let's go, you," he said to Remo and jabbed him with the gun barrel.

Goddamn fool, Remo thought. He had been set up by Dr. Forrester, set up like a schoolchild, set into a trap, and he had walked in like the Redcoat Marching Band, noisily and stupidly.

Crust again brought the phone to his ear as Remo was herded away. At the door, Remo glanced back over his shoulder. Admiral James Benton Crust sat there on his bed, but his hard, piercing eyes were melting into pails of insipid mush. Admiral Crust was listening. And then he was humming. The same tune.

Remo could kick himself. The admiral had known his name. Lithia Forrester must have warned him that Remo was coming. She was calling to check on the results of her handiwork. Now these three sailors were going to have to pay the price.

As they stepped from the admiral's cabin, the sailor Remo had knocked out groaned on the floor. But the other three ignored him and marched Remo along the passageway toward the stairs. The one the admiral had called "chief" still held the gun to the back of Remo's neck as they walked quickly down the stairs to the main deck.

"How'd you get here, Donaldson?" asked the chief. He was not Hollywood's idea of a Navy frogman. He was a pudgy pail of fat with wild, thinning, black curly hair. Remo thought he would have been more at home behind the counter of a candy store in the Bronx than aboard the ship.

"I swam."

"Good swimmer, huh?"

"I can splash around a little."

"How come your clothes aren't wet?"

"They dried. I've been here three hours waiting for my chance."

Remo did not want them to know about the small boat tied up under the bow. He might have use for it yet. And if he were lucky — if they were all lucky — he might not have to kill them.

They were on the main deck now, amidships, and the thin salt air laid a coat of damp on everything. The three men herded Remo along to a side ladder and funneled him down to the water where a small powerboat waited far below.

They sat Remo in the center of the boat. One of the sailors perched on the bow. The chief sat behind Remo, his rifle still at Remo's neck. The third sailor got into the stem of the small launch, pressed the electric starter, and untied the line lashing the boat to the steps.

He opened the throttle and the boat rapidly pulled away from the battleship *Alabama,* heading out into the inky darkness of Chesapeake Bay, toward the shore some four hundred yards away. The lights of houses and buildings twinkled on the shore in silent invitation.

They had gone only about a hundred yards when the motor was cut and the boat began to drift.

"End of the line for you, Donaldson," the chief said.

"Well, that's life," Remo said. "Don't suppose you'd change your mind if I offered to enlist? No, I guess you wouldn't." And then, in a startled voice, Remo called, "What in the hell is that?"

The man perched on the bow was a sailor, not a policeman. He followed Remo's eyes and turned to look out over the bow, and Remo spun his head, sliding it alongside the barrel of the chief's gun. He locked an arm around the chief's blubbery chest and went over the side into the black water, pulling the chief after him. The rifle slid out of the chief's hands and swayed delicately away under the ink-black water.

Chief Petty Officer Benjamin Josephson was a good frogman, although that fact was disguised by his pudgy, bloated shape. He had all the arrogance of a man sure of his skills and it showed in his movements and gestures. His skill in the water had earned him the respect of his men, along with the worthiest kind of respect — his own self-respect.

But he found himself now being treated very disrespectfully with a powerful arm locked around him. With his feet, Remo tried to kick some distance between himself and the boat. As long as he had the chief with him, the sailors in the boat couldn't shoot.

Then Josephson wrapped his hands tightly around Remo's neck. The two of them went under, then surfaced for air. Josephson gulped it down impulsively, like a favorite whiskey, and growled: "Donaldson, you're dead."

"Not yet, swabby," Remo said and then went down again, pulling Josephson deep into the water. Under the cover of the dark water, Remo let Josephson go. Blows were out of the question, so he dug his thumbs into the back of Josephson's hands, crippling the nerves, and slowly Josephson's grip on Remo's neck weakened and then released.

Then they were up again for air and then back down under the surface. Josephson drove his head forward, trying to smash Remo's face, but Remo slid alongside it.

Remo kept his legs moving and they were moving steadily away from the small powerboat. When they surfaced again, Remo could no longer see the boat. And since its motor had not started up again, the two seamen must still be there, still searching the water. Probably, Remo thought, they would be concentrating their search toward the shore. But instead, Remo was kicking and stroking his way back toward the *Alabama*.

He was far enough out of range now. They came up again and Remo pivoted around behind Chief Josephson and locked a powerful forearm around his neck and treaded water to stay in place.

"You want to live?" he hissed into the sailor's ear.

"Go screw yourself, Donaldson. You're a dead man." Josephson started a shout.

Deep in his throat, Remo could feel the rumble and then hear the first sounds: "Hey, men . . ." and then it stopped as Remo muscled his forearm and cut Josephson's air, crushing his Adam's apple back deep into his throat.

"Sorry, fella," Remo said. "Anchors aweigh." He continued to apply pressure until he heard the telltale crack of bones breaking. He released his arm and the chief pitched forward, head-first in the water, began to drift away and down, his stringy, curly hair floating about his head like an inverted Portuguese man-of-war, and then slowly sinking below the surface.

Remo took a deep breath and turned, swimming strongly for the ship. It was still silent behind him; the two sailors must still be searching.

Remo reached the small boat he had tied up at the bow and untied it. He climbed in and pushed himself off from the side of the ship and, using a single oar, began to stroke powerfully toward shore.

Then, behind him, he heard a tremendous roar. His boat bobbed in the water, and through the wooden floor, Remo could feel the ocean vibrating under his feet. He turned and looked back. The battleship *Alabama* had started its engines. Covered now by the roar of the *Alabama*, Remo started his own boat with a pull on the motor cord and began to head back to shore. Halfway there, he saw the battleship's power launch, the two sailors still in it, skidding back toward the battleship, their search abandoned.

Remo shook a chill from his shoulders. So Lithia Forrester had set him up. That was one he owed her, he thought.

Behind him, the powerful engines of the *Alabama* were running strongly now. What was that all about, Remo wondered as he eased himself into the dock. Was the ship going someplace? Was the song that Crust had been humming about to trigger another act of death and destruction?

Twenty

The sun had already risen over the island of Manhattan, illuminating the day's supply of air pollution, when the battleship *Alabama* came lumbering in from the Atlantic toward New York Bay.

Outside the control room, the helmsman was trying to explain something to the officer of the watch.

"I think there's something wrong with him, sir."

"What do you mean?"

"Well, before he chased me out, sir, he was humming all the time."

"Humming?"

"Yes sir."

"What is wrong with humming if the admiral wants to hum?"

"Nothing, sir. But that's not all, sir."

"Oh?"

"I don't know how to say this, sir."

"Well, just say it, man."

"The admiral was . . . well, sir, he was playing with himself."

"What?"

"Playing with himself, sir. You know what I mean."

"You'd better go below, sailor, and check into sick bay," the first officer said. As the sailor walked slowly away, the first officer scratched his head.

Admiral James Benton Crust had indeed been playing with himself. But he had stopped now. He had decided he would rather hum. So he hummed. Sometimes, for a change of pace, he whistled.

And every so often, just so those lazy fakers who didn't really belong in this man's Navy wouldn't forget, he called down to the engine room for "More power. Full speed ahead." Which was odd, since the ship had been at full power since leaving Washington.

Admiral Crust looked around the room, humming, soaking up the feel and tradition of its highly polished wood. The Navy could be a life for a man, if the man were big enough for the Navy. Admiral Crust — master seaman, master diplomat, master lover — was big enough for anything.

Onward, he steamed. To his left, he saw the Kill Van Kull and beyond that, the smoky air hovering over Bayonne's oil refineries. To his right was Brooklyn.

Up ahead loomed Manhattan. The Battery. Its beautiful skyline, beautiful not because of its beauty but because of its magnitude. And up ahead, slightly port of the ship, Liberty Island. The Statue of Liberty held her torch high in the air, her copper plates greened with corrosion, her smile benign as she looked down upon her nation. Behind her back lurked Jersey City, doing all those things that the Statue of Liberty was better off not knowing about.

Admiral Crust picked up the horn again. "More power," he shouted. "You bilge rats produce some power. This is the Navy, man, not an excursion boat. More power."

Down below, in the bowels of the ship, the technicians, who monitored the power plants of a ship of the modern Navy, looked at each other in confusion. "He must think we still have people down here shoveling coal," one said. "Wonder where we are?"

"I don't know," a lieutenant senior grade answered. "But at this speed, we're going to get wherever we're going in a pretty big damn hurry."

Alone in the control room, Admiral James Benton Crust slowly turned the wheel to the left. Gradually, the big ship began to come about toward the port side, veering left, pulling out of its own channel and crossing over the southbound channel. He straightened the wheel. The ship was now on course.

Admiral Crust continued to hum as his big ship steamed ahead toward Liberty Island. The feeling of movement in the sheltered bay was so slight it seemed as if the Statue of Liberty itself were floating on top of the water, racing forward towards his ship.

The thousands of yards separating them quickly turned into hundreds of yards. Crust kept humming. Now he began to jump up and down on the floor of the control room, slapping his hands against his thighs.

"More power," he screamed into the horn. The ship was racing now. The sailboat "Lie-By" capsized in its trail. Two city councilmen out for a ride in a canoe were overturned. An excursion boat headed for the Statute of Liberty saw the battleship *Alabama* bearing down on it. Wisely, the skipper goosed his boat and narrowly got out of the path of the great warship, although two passengers fell overboard in the rocking turbulence that followed the *Alabama* through the water. Overhead, Navy planes that had monitored the cruise of the *Alabama* ever since it had taken off without orders, and all through the night as it refused to respond to radio messages, excitedly relayed reports to a nearby naval air station.

Two hundred yards now and closing fast. Then the heavy battleship crossed out of the continually dredged deep-water channels and its prow began to bite into the mud at the bottom of the bay. But its force and impetus kept it moving forward and the motors continued to scream. Now mud was enveloping the propellers and the ship was no longer cruising, it was sliding, still at full speed, but then it began to slow down as its sharp-edged prow bit more deeply into the mud, but it kept coming and then it crashed into a stone pier, shearing it off from the body of the island like a pat of butter sliced off a warm quarter-pound stick. The ship buckled up against the compacted garbage base of the island — bit its way in, ten, fifteen, then twenty feet, and then stopped, the motors still roaring through the mud, but without effect now.

The ship quivered and pitched over lightly on its side, a sputtering, frustrated behemoth implanted in an island. On the island, park personnel ran about wildly in confusion and shock.

Admiral James Benton Crust left the control room on the dead run, heading for the engine room, far below in the hull of the ship. Seamen were running around in panic, ignoring him.

Some had already jumped overboard onto the island, even though the ship was in no danger of sinking. The whoops of boat sirens could be heard in the air as pleasure boats, then tugs and other commercial vessels in the area, began to ply toward the scene to offer help.

Admiral Crust raced through the now-tilted corridors, oblivious to the excitement, humming to himself, occasionally waving at seamen he recognized.

He entered the engine room.

"All right. All hands, abandon ship."

Seamen began to scurry toward the door.

"You will leave in an orderly manner," the admiral ordered angrily. They slowed their run down to a trot.

The lieutenant senior grade in charge of the engine room saluted: "Admiral, sir. Can I be of assistance?"

"Yes, get out of here."

"Aye aye, sir. And the admiral?"

Crust was even now shoving the lieutenant through the bulkhead door. "The admiral is going to show you jugheads of the modern Navy how a real seaman dies with his ship."

He locked the bulkhead door, spinning the wheel lock, until it was secure. Then, humming to himself, he began to open the sea valves.

Oily, black, muddy water began to pour into the engine room. Clouds of oily putrid steam arose as the water engulfed the huge diesel motors and they sputtered and stopped. Admiral Crust giggled.

"Give me sail, every time, lads, give me sail. Yo, ho, ho, and a bottle of rum."

The young lieutenant pounded on the bulkhead door.

"Admiral, let me in."

Inside, James Benton Crust shouted: "I know what I'm doing. It's the Navy way."

The lieutenant kept pounding for several more minutes. But then there was no one left to hear.

Admiral James Benton Crust, Annapolis '42, was face up, against the metal ceiling of the engine room compartment, the water pressure mashing his face against the steel ceiling plates.

The last thing he did in this world was hum.

Twenty-One

The phone intruded on Remo. He rolled over and pulled his pillow over his head, but still it intruded, an incessant squawking that seemed to get louder with each successive ring.

"Chiun, get the phone," he grumbled. But Chiun had already left their room at the Human Awareness Laboratories for his morning exercise, which consisted primarily of picking flowers.

So, Remo rolled over and snatched the receiver from its cradle.

"Yeah," he snarled.

"Smith here."

"You gone bananas? What the hell are you calling me on this open phone for?"

"It might not matter much longer anyway if we don't get some results. Did you ever hear of an Admiral Crust?"

Remo slid up into a sitting position in bed. "Yeah, I heard of him. Why?"

"This morning he rammed a battleship into the Statue of Liberty. Then he drowned himself in the engine room. He was humming all the way."

"Poor bastard," Remo said. "I was with him last night. I wanted to warn him but I was too late. They had already hooked him."

Remo got to his feet now and was pacing back and forth. Smith said, "With luck, I'll know this afternoon about the bidding."

"Good," Remo said. "I'll call you. I've got some garbage to put out."

"Don't be emotional," Smith said. "Be careful."

"I'm always careful," Remo said, slowly replacing the phone on its stand.

It had been a good trap, he thought, and he had fallen right into it. Sent to kill Admiral Crust; sent into a trap from which he was not supposed to escape. And then Admiral Crust being triggered to run amok. Lithia had not been in her apartment last night when Remo returned. Probably out celebrating the death of Remo Donaldson. No doubt, she believed he was dead . . . as soon *she* would be. Remo Williams was finished playing games.

He was still wearing the salt-stiffened clothes of the night before. He changed rapidly into a fresh shirt and slacks, stepped out into the hall.

It was still early and there were no people in sight. Remo rode the elevator up to the tenth floor. Lithia Forrester's secretary was not yet at her desk and Remo walked past her empty chair, and, without knocking, pushed open the large oak door to enter Lithia Forrester's office.

Her office was bathed brightly in morning sunshine pouring through the overhead dome. But the office was empty. Remo saw a door on the far wall and went through it, into a plush, chrome-and-glass living room. That too was empty.

Remo's trained ears picked up a sound off to the right. He passed through another closed door and was in a bedroom, done all in black. The rug was thick and black; so were the bedspread and drapes. Not even a slice of yellow sunlight slithered into the room around the heavy, lined drapes; the only illumination came from an antique Chinese figurine lamp on the dresser.

The sound he had heard came from the bathroom off the bedroom, the sound of water from a shower, and, merged with it, the sound of a woman singing.

Her voice was melodic and tuneful as she sang the melody: "Super-kali-fragil-istic-expi-ali-docious." She sang the one line over and over again in a high, good-humored kind of chant.

Remo sat on her bed, his eyes toward the slightly opened bathroom door, waiting, thinking that butchers always seemed to enjoy their work. And Lithia Forrester was a butcher. There had been Clovis Porter and General Dorfwill and Admiral Crust. The CIA man Barrett. And how many others had died because of her? How many had Remo himself killed?

Lithia Forrester owed America at least her own life. Remo Williams had come to collect.

The sound of the shower stopped, Lithia Forrester sang more softly to herself now in the bathroom. Remo could imagine her toweling the tall rich body that instilled in every man a satyr's dreams.

He began to whistle the melody. "Super-kali-fragil-istic-expi-ali-docious."

He whistled it louder. She heard it, because she stopped singing and the bathroom door flew open.

Lithia Forrester stood there, naked and golden, the bathroom light from behind her casting an aura around her flaxen hair and peach body.

She was smiling in anticipation, but then she saw Remo sitting on her bed, only eight feet away, and she stopped. Her eyes widened in horror and fright. Her mouth hung open.

"Expecting someone else?" Remo said.

Then she was embarrassed. She turned her body slightly away from Remo and thrust an arm across her breasts.

"Too late to be shy," Remo said. "Remember? I turned off your lights last night? I've come to do it again."

Lithia paused, then dropped her arm and turned her full body toward Remo. "I remember, Remo. I remember. You did turn off my lights. And it was never better. I want you to do it again. Right now. Right here."

She walked forward until she was only inches from Remo. His face was at the level of her waist. She reached behind his head and pulled him forward until his face was buried against her soft, still-damp belly.

"What did you do last night, Remo?" she asked. "After you left me."

"If you mean did I kill Admiral Crust as you told me to, no. Did I fall into the trap you set for me and get killed by Crust's men, no. Did I stop Crust from ramming his ship today into the Statue of Liberty, no." He spoke softly, as if confiding a secret to her stomach. He reached his hands slowly around her back, resting them on her firm smooth cheeks, and then he reached both hands up and grabbed two handfuls of long blond hair and yanked her head back with a snap.

He jumped to his feet and spun Lithia Forrester around and tossed her onto the bed.

"I got cheated all around, sweetheart. And now I'm back for a refund."

She lay on the bed, momentarily frightened. Then she slid one leg up and turned slightly onto her side, a white pool of sensuality on the blackness of the bed. "Shall I wrap it or will you have it here?" she asked with a smile. Her teeth made her skin look dark. She reached her arms up toward Remo invitingly and her breasts rose toward him, pointed and inviting. Then Remo was over her and then he joined her.

He had never seen a more beautiful woman, Remo thought, as he paused over her before their bodies melted together in a confluence of passion.

And then Lithia Forrester was a dervish, bucking and rocking spastically under Remo, and Remo had no chance to do to her all the things he wanted to do, because he was too busy hanging on.

She hissed and groaned and gyrated her way across the bed in a passion that was curiously without passion and then, from the corner of his eye, Remo saw her arm reach up to the bedside end table and fumble in the drawer and come out with a pair of scissors.

Remo was filled with fury at this woman who killed remorselessly and in whom he had not found a spark of honest passion or love, and he began to grind her down, matching her artificial frenzy with an even greater frenzy of his own — a frenzy of hatred. Then she was pressed up against the headboard. Remo ploughed on, inexorably, and she was moaning, but it was a moan of pain, not pleasure. Behind his back, she joined both her hands on the handle of the scissors and raised her arms high in the air over Remo's broad back.

Then she brought her hands down, scissors point first, as Remo slid out from under her arms. The scissors whizzed past the top of his head and buried themselves deeply in Lithia Forrester's chest.

She felt too much shock to feel pain. Then a look of blank stupidity crossed her face and she looked at Remo with kind of a quizzical hurt in her eyes as he pulled away from her. He watched the blood send trails down the sides of her golden body as the handle of the scissors throbbed cruelly in the light from the single lamp, shuddering with each weak beat of her dying heart.

"That's what I meant by turning off your lights, sweetheart," Remo said and backed away to stand at the bottom of the bed, watching Lithia Forrester die. He anointed her going by whistling:

"Super-kali-fragil-istic-expi-ali-docious."

Twenty-Two

Dr. Harold K. Smith sat behind his desk at Folcroft Sanitarium, his back to the piles of papers, and stared out the one-way glass at the calm waters of Long Island Sound, waiting for the telephone to ring.

Since CURE had been founded years before to help equalize the fight against crime, Folcroft had been its secret headquarters. Now Smith found himself wondering how secret it still was. Some of its security had been breached; the attack on Remo had proved that. Unless Remo were successful, there was no way to tell just how high up that breach might have occurred. Smith shuddered at the thought, but it could have come right from the Oval Office of the White House.

If that were the case, there was an aluminum box down in the basement in which Harold K. Smith was ready to lock himself; to take to his grave all the secrets of a nation's last desperate fight against crime and chaos.

Unless Remo somehow could remove the threat; unless the Destroyer could again make America safe against those overseas forces who would buy its government to turn it to their own ends.

But why didn't the telephone ring?

Harold K. Smith, the only director CURE ever had, expected three calls and he wanted only two of them. The one from Switzerland and the one from Remo. The third? Well, he would worry about that when it came.

The phone rang and Smith spun around, hearing the squeak of the chair and telling himself to be sure to have it oiled. He picked up the phone and said, with no trace of emotion or haste:

"Smith."

119

It was one of the calls he wanted. A CURE division chief who thought he worked for the U.S. Bureau of Narcotics had finally heard from a friend in Switzerland who had been talking to his own friend, a ski instructor. And the ski instructor had told how his prize pupil, a young American secretary to a Swiss banker, was flying back to New York today. But she expected to be coming back right away because she had return tickets for tomorrow night.

The CURE division chief who thought he worked for the Bureau of Narcotics thought the Swiss banker was probably a narcotics courier and he asked Smith: "Should I have him picked up at the airport?"

"No," Smith said. "Just have customs wave him through."

"But . . ."

"No buts," Smith said. "Wave him through." He hung up the phone and turned again to the window. That jibed with information they had received from diplomatic sources about chiefs of intelligence coming to the United States under false names, supposedly assigned to the United Nations missions. They would also arrive today? CURE had learned they would be leaving tomorrow night. That meant the auction would be tomorrow. But where?

Tomorrow. Time was running out . . . running out on CURE, running out on Remo Williams, running out on America.

Dr. Smith watched the waters of Long Island Sound lap at the rocks in front of his windows and ate his frustration. With time running out, all he could do was wait. Wait and hope.

It was almost noon when the telephone rang again. Again, Smith spun and lifted the receiver.

"Smith."

"Remo," the voice said. "She's dead."

"The auction's tomorrow," Smith said.

"Where?"

"I don't know," Smith said. "If she's dead, will that cancel it?"

"Afraid not," Remo said. "She was in it with somebody."

"Who?"

"I don't know yet. I'm still looking."

"Then we really haven't accomplished anything," Smith said, with a sinking feeling in the pit of his stomach.

"Don't worry about it, Smitty. We'll tie it up with a bow by tomorrow. And leave the auction to me. I'll take care of it."

120

"All right, Remo. We're counting on you. Keep in touch."

Smith felt buoyed by confidence after talking to Remo, even thought he did not see how even Remo could bring the whole scheme crashing down.

He stood up behind his desk, anxious to leave his office, to escape the third phone call — the unwanted call — when the phone rang.

With a sigh of resignation but with the decisiveness built by a life's habit of doing his duty, Smith picked up the telephone.

"Smith," he said, then listened as a nervous voice poured out its worries and frustrations.

"Yes, I understand," Smith said.

"Yes, I understand."

Finally, he said, "Don't worry about it, Mr. President. We will have everything in hand."

Then he hung up. How could he tell the president the truth? How? When there was no guarantee that the president himself was not under the power of the strange mind-corruptors?

Smith sat down again, deciding against lunch, and began to bury himself and his worries in routine paperwork, to hope against hope that Remo Williams could act in time.

For all his confidence on the telephone, Remo was stumped. He had gone through Lithia Forrester's office files three times and had found nothing. He sat in Dr. Forrester's chair behind her desk, secure behind the locked oaken doors, papers strewn all across her desk.

Finally, in frustration and anger, he swiped all the papers off the desk, brushing them onto the floor.

He looked over the desk to the couch where Lithia Forrester's secretary lay, bound and gagged. She had come into the office shortly after 9 A.M. and found Remo rifling through the file cabinets near Dr. Forrester's desk.

Instead of screaming and running, she had demanded to know what he was doing. For her trouble, she was tapped unconscious, gagged, and tied up on the couch.

Remo had found his and Chiun's files. Nothing. Test results; Dr. Forrester's observations about Remo who had aggressive fantasies. Zero. No file on Dorfwill or Porter or Barrett or Bannon.

There must be a private file, Remo thought. The secretary should know where it is.

He stood up from the desk and walked over to the couch, the secretary's frightened green eyes blinking with every one of his steps. It would have been impossible for Lithia Forrester to find a woman who could outshine her, but she had tried. The secretary was a statuesque redhead, and as Remo stood over her and looked into those deep green eyes, he could tell that she was a woman, a real woman, unlike the dead excuse for one on Lithia Forrester's bed.

The secretary's arms were tied behind her back, wrapped around and around with Scotch tape Remo had found on the desk, and her arms, pulled back, swelled her rich breasts out in front through the thin green sweater she wore.

Remo sat on the edge of the couch and thrust his hand under her sweater, resting it on her bare abdomen. He could feel her skin tingle under his touch. It would be easy, if only she knew something.

"Do you know who I am?" he asked.

She nodded.

"Do you know why I'm here?"

She shook her head.

"I'm a murderer," he said, enjoying the shock in her eyes. "Haven't you ever seen my files? You should know that."

She shook her head.

"Where is my file?" he asked.

She pointed her eyes toward the filing cabinets behind the desk, then looked back at Remo.

"It's not in there," he lied. "Where else does Dr. Forrester keep her files?"

The secretary shrugged and shook her head.

Remo snaked his hand up under her sweater and fixed it on one of her pendulous breasts. The breast was overrated as an erogenous zone, but there were nerves that worked. He began to press with his fingers against the nerves of her breast and he leaned his face over, close to hers.

"Think again. Where does she keep the rest of her files?"

With his free hand, Remo flipped loose the gag around the girl's mouth and then covered her lips with his own before she could scream. His other hand worked her breast. Despite herself, she became aroused.

If she had had any inclination to scream, it was lost in her return of Remo's kiss and in the workings of his meandering hand. Finally, he pulled his face away slightly: "It's important," he said. "Where are Dr. Forrester's other files?"

"Some patient files are confidential," the girl said. "I'll be fired if I tell you."

Remo kissed her again, gently. "Not by Dr. Forrester," he said. "She's dead."

"Dead?"

"I killed her," Remo said and again covered the redhead's lips with his own. His right hand now traced spirals around her breast, pausing to pinch nerves. He freed her mouth again and looked at her hard:

"I need those files. Nothing can stop me."

The warming fires of her own passion had weakened her and the harsh cruelty of Remo's words crushed her.

"In the bedroom closet," she said. "A safe built into the wall. But I don't have a key."

"That's okay," Remo said and kissed her again. As he kissed her, he transferred his hand from her breast to her neck and squeezed slightly on a major blood vessel. The girl passed out, smiling.

Remo refastened the gag and went into the bedroom, ignoring the dead body of Lithia Forrester sprawled on the bed, the blood now hardening along its courses down the sides of her body, her eyes still open wide with shock and fear. The scissors had stopped quivering.

It wasn't much of a safe. Remo worked the lock until it snapped off under the side of his hand. He inserted a finger through the opening, popped the latch from the inside. The heavy door swung free and Remo pulled it open.

There were three racks of red cardboard folders and Remo made three trips to carry them all back out into Lithia Forrester's sun-bright office, where he stacked them neatly on the floor against a file cabinet.

They were numbered in order, starting with number 1. Remo placed the first folder carefully in front of him on the now-clear desk, unsure of what he was looking for, not knowing what he might find.

He found nothing. It was another patient file, just like the hundreds of others in the file cabinets Remo had rifled, this time on an assistant secretary of defense. A pile of test papers from the psychological battery that all new patients underwent. Then a page of notes handwritten on a yellow sheet in pencil in the small handwriting of a woman. Remo read the notes. Psychological drivel. Repressed feelings of aggression. Unhappy childhood. Resentment of authority. He grimaced to himself. Why did everybody's problems sound alike in the hands of a shrink?

The file numbered 2 was the same. A Treasury Department official. More psychological problems.

Remo began to go through the folders more quickly. Number 3, number 4, number 5. All the same. Government officials. Test results. Lithia Forrester's impressions. Remo began grabbing them by the handful now, placing the hard red folders on the desk before him, flipping quickly through the sheets they contained.

Mountains of information — yet nothing Remo could use.

He stood up, exhaling almost in a sigh, and walked from behind the desk, padding softly back and forth across the deep pile rug.

The folders must have the answer. But where was it? Now Remo knew what government officials she had under her control. That was something. But how did she do it? Who was her partner — that person she had talked to last night as Remo lay on her couch?

Keep looking.

Remo sat down again behind the desk and pulled another batch of red folders off the floor. More names. More government officials. More test results. More written analyses.

A Who's Who of American government. Top policy makers. Cabinet officers. Security people. Nothing to help Remo.

Folder number 71. Number 72. Number 73.

And then there was one more folder.

It was the last one and it was not numbered. Remo opened it. No test results this time. Six pages in Lithia Forrester's crabbed handwriting, six pages listing names of government officials. Remo skimmed the first page and groaned to himself — they were the same names he had just gone through.

Read carefully.

Each name was numbered, and next to each name were the man's government title, his telephone numbers, and a column labeled "fee schedule."

Remo whistled to himself. Some paid $200 a day, which included $100 for 50 minutes of private time. And the government was picking up a lot of the tabs. No wonder the nation was $400 billion in debt.

But under each entry was another line. It read "Potential." The number 1 name was the assistant secretary of defense. "Potential: leak of secrets; falsification of documents."

Number 2 was the Treasury officer. "Potential: security problems on Fort Knox gold."

Remo read the list rapidly. All the names were there. All the things that Lithia Forrester could get them to do. Things to cripple America.

Burton Barrett. Potential: exposure of CIA agents.

Bannon. Potential: investigation; force if needed.

Dorfwill. Potential: bombing incident.

That was it. Down through all the names, through all six sheets of paper, Lithia Forrester had marked what they could be counted on to do.

From number 1 through number 72.

Remo sighed, then carefully folded the sheets and put them in his right hip pocket. Smith could use that. 72 officials who had been compromised by Lithia Forrester. There might be more than that, but at least Remo had 72.

72?

Remo glanced at the red file folders near him on the desk, then shuffled through them quickly with his hand. He found the one he was looking for. It was number 73. The folders had gone up to 73, but the list had only 72 names.

Who was missing?

He took the list from his pocket and ran his finger down the handwritten lists of names again.

The list was in alphabetical order. Bannon . . . Barrett . . . more names . . . Dorfwill . . . more names . . . Fs . . . Gs. And a name was missing.

And Remo knew which one it was.

He went digging through the red patient folders until he saw the one he wanted and opened it.

He had only skimmed it before, not even looking, just assuming it was more test papers and more analysis of problems.

The folder contained that. But it contained more too. Detailed notes of the whole scheme. The secret of the humming. How Lithia had controlled her victims. All in the folder belonging to Lithia Forrester's partner — or, as it turned out while Remo read it, to her lover and boss. The man who had put together the scheme to sell America.

Remo pulled the pages from the folder and placed them with the list of 72 names. He refolded them carefully, and again put them into his back pocket. With a swipe of his arm, he knocked the other file folders all over the floor, clearing the desk. He kicked his way through the folders, papers splashing, their contents hopelessly jumbled.

He walked from behind the desk and paused at the side of the secretary on the couch. She was just coming to and he leaned over her.

"Just try to be comfortable, honey. Later on, I'll send someone up to free you. And I hope we get a chance to meet again sometime." He leaned over and kissed her on the eyelids and then, with his hands, put her to sleep again.

He had work to do.

Twenty-Three

Remo paused outside the door of the room on the sixth floor, reserved for patients at the Human Awareness Laboratory.

The other patients' doors were plain gray with shiny metal handles. These doors were black. Highly polished black doors. A passerby might think the room did not belong to a patient. Perhaps the passerby might be correct.

Remo paused in front of the door when he heard the periodic thwack, thwack, thwack. The sound was familiar but he could not place it.

Other patients' doors had no locks. But these black double doors had a central bolt, the worst kind of lock for a double door. Any grown man, with a little forward pressure, could ease the bolt out of its slot. Remo did it with a snap of his forefinger.

The doors sprung open. Standing in a very large, plush room was a mountain of nude chocolate, its back to Remo. The head on the mountain spun around with the wheezing of an asthmatic who had exercised too much.

"Get out of here," said Dr. Lawrence Garrand, the world's foremost authority on atomic waste disposal. "I'm busy."

Garrand stood, his bare brown feet sunk into a plush white polar bear rug, his two dark rolling arms containing an avalanche of flesh, at the end of which were two almost-pointed hands holding darts.

Garrand did not move his body around because it would take several steps to accomplish. Instead, he kept his head twisted over his sloping shoulders where the cascade of flesh seemed to begin. Large white stretch marks cut his billowing buttocks into a road map. The legs looked like dried lava flows defying the law of gravity, as if the polar bear rug had vomited up the dark mass.

Yet the face underneath the flesh, the face that turned over the shoulder to glare at Remo, was a delicate, fine face.

Remo could catch a glint on the flesh of the forehead from a diffused overhead light. Garrand was perspiring. Yet the room was cool and smelled of delicate mint incense. Garrand's perspiration came apparently from the exertion of his dart-throwing.

"Get out of here," Garrand wheezed.

Remo stepped into the room, never feeling so light in his life. Two steps into the room, he saw what Garrand's target was, what his body had been hiding, like a mountain obscuring a view of a valley.

There was Lithia Forrester, about a third larger than life-size, in full golden color, naked, seated on a purple cushion, one leg folded up in front of her and the other extended full, exposing her to view. Holes punctured the blue eyes, and the erogenous zones were perforated with the memory of thousands of darts. Three red-feathered darts protruded from her navel.

All the while, from the portrait, Lithia smiled seductively, the even, white smile of cool confidence and joy.

Remo looked back to Garrand.

Around his neck, the world's foremost authority on atomic waste disposal had hung his asthma spray bulb on a leather thong. A fold of flesh had hidden the leather thong from the back.

Garrand's eyes followed Remo as Remo moved into the room, and just the movement of his head set his body quivering. His breasts were larded with white streaks like an overboiled hot dog just before splitting. Fat fought fat for space fore and aft on his arms. His nipples were bigger than Lithia's.

He squeezed his asthma bulb into his mouth, squirting his bronchial tubes with adrenaline.

"I thought I told you to get out of here," he said.

"I heard you," Remo said.

Garrand shrugged, a very slight shrug that made his flesh ripple. He dropped the spray back onto his rolling stomach, and turned his head again toward Lithia's picture.

Garrand raised a dart to precise eye level with his right hand. The left hand still held two more. With a flick of his fingers, Garrand let loose a dart as he announced:

"Left breast."

The dart thwacked in just over the aureole around Lithia Forrester's nipple.

"Right nipple," Garrand said and powerfully, almost invisibly, with no curve in its trajectory, another dart flashed across the eight-foot distance and buried itself, quivering, in the turgid right nipple of Lithia Forrester.

"Mons veneris," Garrand said, and the third dart flashed on too, punching its way into the triangular patch of golden hair on the portrait.

Garrand reached down to a wooden dart box and took out three more darts. "You haven't told me why you busted in here."

"The game's over, Garrand."

"So the bitch talked."

"No, she didn't, if that's any consolation to you. She died without saying a word."

"Good for her. I knew the honky bitch was good for something. Right eye," he said and buried a dart into the sparkling blue eye of Lithia Forrester.

"Mouth," he called, and another dart hit its mark with a thwack.

"Why, Garrand?" Remo asked. "Just because of a traffic arrest in Jersey City?"

"Vagina," Garrand called and buried another dart in the exposed private parts of Lithia Forrester. "Not just because of a traffic arrest, Donaldson. Just because your country is rotten. It deserves what it gets. And I deserve whatever I can get for it. Call it back-dues to my people." He was wheezing now from the exertion of talking so long.

"Your people?" Remo said. "What about your people whose lives would be ruined if your scheme worked?"

"That's the tough luck associated with being a house nigger," Garrand said. "Listen. As long as you're there, give me more darts, will you. On that table. In the box."

Remo had reached a waist-high white table with a marble top, an exquisite piece of furniture that went with the exquisite room, mostly furnished in white. On the tabletop was a black box, the size of a loaf of bread, with layer after layer of darts in it, like bombs in a storage hangar. Remo grabbed three by their heavy metal points. The feathers were trimmed and true. The points sharp. The wooden bodies were weighted, about a fifth of an ounce heavier than competition darts.

He handed the darts to Garrand who accepted them. Then Remo stepped back, eight feet away from Garrand.

"Left thumb," Garrand said, and flew a dart into Lithia Forrester's left thumb.

"Whose idea was it?" Remo asked. "Yours or hers?"

"Mine, of course. She didn't have brains enough to think of it." He turned now, shuffling and labored, to face Remo. "But I saw the possibilities as soon as I came here for therapy and saw all the government personnel here. I thought right away of the kind of power she could have over them. She could get them to do anything."

"How'd you get her to do it?" Remo asked.

"You might not believe it, Donaldson, but she loved me."

"So you used drugs and posthypnotic suggestion?"

"To simplify it for you, yes. Plus Lithia's peddling her ass. That helped. Men were just fascinated by her body. A little of her twiff and they'd do anything," Garrand said imperiously. He was lecturing now. "I never could understand it myself. She just wasn't that good."

"I thought you couldn't get someone to act against their will under hypnosis," Remo said.

"A typical piece of comic-book stupidity," Garrand said. "First you convince them that what they're doing is the right thing to do. That colonel, for instance. He thought you were a Russian spy. And General Dorfwill. He wasn't bombing St. Louis; he was bombing Peking in retaliation for a sneak attack. And Admiral Crust? Why shouldn't he try to destroy the Statue of Liberty, particularly since he knew it was the hideout for a band of anarchists about to blow up our country? That's how it's done, Mr. Donaldson."

"And the song?"

"That was my idea, too," Garrand said, smiling, his teeth pearled in the ground-coffee brownness of his face. "You've got to be careful when you use trigger words to set a person off. You can't pick a word that someone's liable to hear in conversation. It could set them off before you were ready. When you think about it, not many people are likely to use super-kali-fragil-istic-expi-ali-docious in conversation."

"A lovely plan," Remo said. "I respect you for it. Now I need to know where the bidding will be held."

Garrand smiled and ignored the question. "One thing puzzles me, Donaldson. I had everything worked out. All except you. This government isn't that good that one of our sources shouldn't have a line on you. It's like all of a sudden there was an organization that did not exist. But it existed. And so did you. Now, if you wish to live, if you wish these darts not to enter your eyes or your temples or wherever I wish, you can tell me where you came from."

Remo laughed. "You lose," he said. He saw his laughter grate Dr. Garrand like a rasp and then the two pointy hands flicked and the darts were at him in that flat trajectory, across the eight feet of room, but Remo's head did not move. His eyes, toward which the darts flew, did not blink. Remo's hands flashed up in front of his face and his hands caught the darts by the points, between thumb and index finger; hands receiving the thrust of the killer weights, wrists like spring locks accepting the force and holding. Short, just short of the eyes.

Garrand's mouth opened. His eyes widened. He looked toward the box of darts on the table and querulously reached forward a hand. But suddenly his hand was pinned to the table as Remo pierced it with one of the darts. "Right thumb," Remo said. He still held the other dart in his right hand.

For the first time in years, Garrand became physical. He ripped his hand loose from the dart, tearing the flesh, and lumbered toward Remo. And for the first time in years, he felt his legs going high above him, above his head, and he was up at the diffused lighting, then at the walls, and than his head was buried in the polar bear rug, and there was that arrogant white face between his bare feet, and Lawrence Garrand was upside down, his head pressed painfully into the rug. He had scarcely seen the man move. And it was becoming hard to breathe.

"Okay, sweetheart," said the leering face between his feet. "Where's the auction?"

Garrand breathed in and tried to breathe out. It was getting more difficult. The blood was pouring into his head and his chocolate skin was taking on a blood-gorged purple color. He fought to exhale. His chest pressed down into his chin. A strand of polar-bear hair caught in his eye and burned.

"Where's the auction?" that white face insisted, then began to press down on Garrand's legs, forcing them into his waist, and Garrand finally blurted out, "Villebrook Equity Associates. New York. Tomorrow." He was exhausted from the effort.

"Okay, sweetheart," Remo said. "Time to go bye-bye."

"You can't kill me," Garrand insisted. "I'm the foremost authority on atomic waste disposal. I deserve to live."

"Sure. So did Clovis Porter. General Dorfwill. A lot of others."

"Call the police then," Garrand gasped. "You can't kill me. If I were white, you wouldn't kill me."

"I'd kill you in any color, sweetheart." Remo looked down along Garrand's wet brown body and his eyes met those of the world's foremost authority on atomic waste disposal. Remo extended the remaining dart out over Garrand's face with his right hand. "External jugular," he called, then dropped the dart. It buried itself into the flesh alongside Garrand's throat, and a thin purple spurt of blood fountained out of his neck as the blood pressure was momentarily relieved by the pierced vein. Remo dropped Garrand heavily to the floor. Before Remo turned off his breath forever, Garrand managed to gasp something muffled by the fat folds of his cheeks and chin. Later, Remo would think that what he said was "I knew it wouldn't work. You people . . ."

Twenty-Four

When Remo returned to his room, Chiun was sitting rigidly in the lotus position, staring at the television.

Remo opened his mouth to speak and Chiun raised a hand for silence.

Only seconds later, organ music up and over, Chiun leaned forward and turned off the television.

"Good afternoon, Little Father," Remo said. "Have you had a pleasant day?"

"Relatively, my son, although I must admit I weary of telling that blighted mass of womanhood that she is indeed loved. And you?"

"Very productive. We must leave now."

"Our work is finished?" Chiun asked.

"Our work here is finished. We have other tasks to perform elsewhere."

"I will be ready to leave in moments," Chiun said.

He was, and Remo realized that his uncharacteristic haste was fueled by his desire to get back to their Washington hotel room and recover his TV-taping machine to record the shows he was now missing.

But they stopped at the hotel only long enough to pay their bill and for Remo to slip the bell captain $100 to ship their luggage to a nonexistent address in Avon-by-the-Sea on the Jersey Shore. And then they were back in their rented convertible on their way to Dulles Airport outside Washington.

Chiun grumbled all the way at the idiocy of leaving a perfectly good television recorder behind and finally extracted a promise from Remo that he could buy another in New York that night.

And later that night, after they checked into a midtown Manhattan hotel, Chiun insisted upon Remo's giving him $500 so he could buy one, which he did, along with five new robes, a pocketknife, and a whistle. The latter two were to protect himself on New York's crime-ridden streets, he explained.

They both rose early the next morning and Chiun worked with Remo on his balance and rhythm, setting out strings of drinking glasses across the floor and having Remo race across the tops of them, barefooted, at increasing speeds.

Remo felt good. He could taste the end of this assignment. After he showered and shaved, he dressed, reluctantly donning the polka-dot tie he had brought with him. If he was going to take part in the bidding for America, he should look the part, he told his image in the mirror. He buttoned his new double-breasted dark blue suit.

Before leaving, he entrusted Lithia Forrester's lists to Chiun, telling him: "Until you hear from me, guard these with your life."

Chiun was deep in his morning meditation and only grunted, but that meant he understood. The lists lay on the floor in front of Chiun where Remo had placed them as Remo went out of their room.

In a men's store off the lobby, Remo bought a conservative regimental striped tie and dropped the other into an ash-bucket near the desk.

In the telephone book, he looked up the address and number of Villebrook Equity Associates, then dialed.

A woman's voice answered and Remo told her he was an investor who wanted someone to propose a tax shelter for him. Could he make an appointment to see someone right away?

"Not today, sir, I'm afraid. Our offices will be closed from noon until 3 P.M. I could make you an appointment for tomorrow."

"That's a strange way to run a business," Remo said.

"Well, frankly, sir, the building is a little run down and we are having an exterminator in."

"And there'll be no one there at all?" Remo asked.

"Only Mr. Bogeste, our treasurer and founder. But he'll be keeping an eye on the exterminator. He won't be able to see anyone."

"Okay," Remo said. "Thank you. I'll call tomorrow."

He hung up the phone. That was it. Right after noon, with all the workers out of the office, the bidding would be held. He hoped they had room for one more.

* * *

Remo was in the eighth-floor hall outside the offices of Villebrook Equity Associates shortly after noon, when a dozen workers poured out from the glass doors, delighted at the prospect of a three-hour lunch, paid for by the company.

Behind them, a young, athletic-looking man with long black hair cast a quizzical glance at Remo, then closed and locked the door from the inside.

The crowd of workers took the elevator down, but Remo hung around the elevator door, as if waiting for an empty car. Minutes later, he heard a phone ring down the hall. It stopped ringing abruptly, and then, after no more than 60 seconds, another door down the hall opened and eight men walked down the hallway toward Remo. He pressed impatiently on the elevator button, but glanced at the men as they passed. It looked like a United Nations caucus, Remo thought, the men almost carrying on their faces the flags of their native countries. Did he look as American as they looked foreign? Remo wondered.

The men walked past the main entrance of Villebrook Equity Associates and through a second door, which was unlocked. Remo could hear it click shut behind them.

The elevator stopped again but Remo shook his head at the old woman in it who was riding down. "I'm going to wait for an empty one so I can get a seat," he said pleasantly and kicked his foot past the electric eye to activate the door, which closed quietly on the confused old lady.

Remo waited for almost five minutes and then went to the door the men had entered. He pressed his ear to the door but could hear, only faintly, the mumbled buzz of voices. They must be in another office beyond this one, he thought. Remo quietly tested the knob. The door was locked.

He went back to the double glass door marked VILLEBROOK EQUITY ASSOCIATES, and with a coin from his pocket tapped lightly on the glass. He was sure that Mr. Bogeste would be guarding the front door.

He tapped again, very softly, and then the door, fastened by a chain lock, opened slightly and the young man he had seen before peered out.

"Mister Bogeste?" Remo said.

"Yes?"

"I'm the exterminator," Remo said. He shot his left hand through the door opening and grabbed Bogeste's Adam's apple between his fingers. With his right hand, be quietly wrenched the chain from the door and stepped inside.

He locked the door behind him and, still holding Bogeste by the windpipe, pushed him back into a leather secretarial chair.

He leaned over and whispered to him: "You like your children?"

Bogeste nodded.

"No more than I do," Remo said. "It'd be a pity if they had to grow up without a father. So why don't you just sit here and think about them?" With his right hand, he pressed a vein behind Bogeste's ear and soon the blood drained from Bogeste's face and he passed out.

He would be good for at least twenty minutes, Remo knew. Long enough to accomplish his business.

Remo followed his ears. He went past a bank of secretary's desks, then right into a hallway that opened on two small private offices. At the end of the hallway, a door was ajar and light beamed from within. Remo walked quietly to the door and listened to the voices inside.

A cultured voice, European but not British, spoke in English. "You gentlemen all know the rules now and agree to them. I will now receive your sealed bids and I will open them in another room. I will return to announce the successful bidder. The others may leave and next week may pick up their nation's good-faith deposits at my office in Zurich. I will arrange with the successful bidder to speak with my principal and to transfer the gold and the information. Is that clear?"

There was a polyglot rumble of assents around the table. Da, ja, oui, yes, sí.

"May I have your envelopes, please?" the first voice said again.

Remo heard a rustle of papers, and then a chair slid along the floor. "I will now go inside to inspect the bids."

"Choost a moment, Mr. Rentzel," came a guttural voice. "How do we know that you will report the truth? Will you tell us the amount of the successful bid?"

"To answer your second question first, no, I will not announce the amount of the successful bid, since the raising of it will be a matter of some delicacy for the country involved. Knowledge of the amount might hinder those efforts. And in answer to your first question, would it not have been foolish to bring everybody here to bid if we had already agreed in advance to sell it to one specific country? Finally, sir, I might point out that the House of Rapfenberg is involved in these negotiations, and we would not be a party to a fraud under any circumstances. Are there any other questions?"

There was silence, and then Remo heard footsteps walking toward the doorway near which he stood. He softly darted back into one of the private offices that opened off the narrow hallway, ready to collar the man from behind if necessary.

But the footsteps turned into the office in which Remo stood, and as the man flipped the light switch and walked in, Remo softly closed the door behind him.

The man heard the door close and turned, startled to see Remo standing there.

"Who the hell are you?" asked Amadeus Rentzel of the House of Rapfenberg.

"I'd like to borrow money to buy a used car," Remo said.

"This office is closed. Get out of here before I call the police."

"Well, if you won't lend me money for a car, I'll buy something else. Maybe a government. Got any governments for sale?"

Rentzel shrugged. "I don't know what you're talking about."

"I'll make it clearer then. I've come to bid."

"From what nation?" Rentzel asked cautiously. "And why hasn't your country placed its good-faith deposit?"

"From the United States of America," Remo said. "From the land of Clovis Porter, General Dorfwill, Burton Barrett, and Admiral Crust. My bid is their lives and we have already paid in full. No other deposit is required."

Rentzel stared for a moment into Remo's eyes. He met and measured the hardness there, then rejected the possibility that Remo was a crank or a bluffer. Rentzel had stared down too many men across the table to be fooled.

He knew it; it was all over.

Rentzel took the news like a Swiss banker. He sat back lightly against the edge of the desk and ran a finger down a knife-edge crease in his trousers. "What of my principal?" he asked. "The man I represent."

"Dead," Remo said.

"What kind of man was he?" Rentzel asked. "I never saw him."
"He was a mad dog. He died like a mad dog," Remo said.
"And what will happen to me?"
"I have no desire to kill you, Mr. Rentzel," Remo said. "After today, I think you should return to Switzerland and spend the rest of your career doing what bankers are meant to do: fleecing widows and orphans, embezzling funds from estates, borrowing money at 5 percent to lend at 18 percent."

Rentzel shrugged and smiled. "As you would have it. Shall I go back in and tell them the auction is over?"

"No," Remo said. "Some pleasures I reserve for myself." Suddenly, his hand darted out. The knuckle of a bent thumb tapped lightly against Rentzel's temple; the Swiss banker fell back heavily on the desk, unconscious.

Remo eased the envelopes from Rentzel's hand and left the office. He walked down the hall, pushed open the door, then walked into a large walnut-panelled conference room.

Seven pairs of eyes turned to meet him as he entered, and when they saw it was not Rentzel, there was a murmured buzz of conversation. An Oriental said, "Where is Mr. Rentzel?"

"He is out for a while," Remo said as he walked to the head of the table. "I am empowered to complete his business."

He stood at the head of the long glass-topped table, meeting the eyes individually, one after another, of the men who sat along the sides of the table.

"Before I announce the successful bidder," he said, "I would like to make several points pertaining to this auction."

He leaned forward on the table with his fists, one hand still holding the batch of envelopes he had taken from Rentzel.

"It was announced that the initial bid would be in gold," Remo said. "But the successful bidder has bid more than gold. He has also bid in courage and in blood and in dedication. In the courage to stand against the forces of evil; in the blood spilled to open a new land; in the dedication to endure and to be true to the ideals of freedom and liberty for all men.

"Gentlemen, the successful bidder is the United States of America."

There were shouts of protest and outrage around the table. Men looked at other men. A man who had to be a Russian, because no one else would wear such a suit, stood up and pounded on the table. "We will double our bid."

"So will we," said the Oriental. "Anything to prevent control of the United States from passing into the hands of these revisionist pigs," he said, staring at the Russian across the table.

Another babble of angry voices broke out and Remo halted it by pounding on the table. "The bidding is closed, gentlemen," he said coldly, "and all of you have lost."

He looked around at each in turn. "Now I would suggest you all return where you came from because in five minutes I am going to call the Federal Bureau of Investigation.

"If you are still here when they arrive, it might be embarrassing for your nations. And when you return home, tell your governments that the United States will never be for sale. If they want the United States, they must come bearing arms."

Remo stood back and waved his envelope-laden hand toward the door. "Leave now, gentlemen, while you're still able to. I will hold these bids for whatever use they will be to the government of the United States. Now leave."

Grumbling but defeated, they got slowly to their feet and, talking angrily with each other, passed through the door and began to leave the office.

Remo sat back down at the table, looking at the envelopes in his hands. How much was the United States worth to its enemies? Or to its friends? He tore the corner off one of the envelopes, then shook his head. One more thing he was better off not knowing. Smith could take care of it.

The sounds had died down and the office of Villebrook Equity Associates was silent.

Remo stood up and walked out into the hallway. As he passed the small office, he saw Amadeus Rentzel still on the desk. He would be coming to shortly.

And in the outer office, the Villebrook man was stirring. Remo smiled. The man had kids. He was happy he hadn't had to kill him.

Twenty-Five

It was after two o'clock when Remo returned to his hotel room. Chiun was fussing with his tape recorder when Remo entered, but Chiun turned and greeted him with warmth. The papers Remo had entrusted to his care were still on the floor where Remo had placed them.

"Why all the pleasantness?" Remo asked suspiciously.

"You had the look in your eyes today of a man with an awful mission. I am glad you have returned safe, full of accomplishment and nastiness."

"We're not out of the woods yet," Remo said.

He lifted the phone and got a local dial tone from the operator and dialed the toll-free number that from anywhere would reach Smith's desk.

The phone was picked up on the first ring.

"Smith."

"Remo. Someday I'm going to call and you're not going to be at your desk and I'm going to tell the Bureau of Antiquities — or whoever's payroll you're on — to dock you for the time."

"Save the chatter," Smith said. "What happened?"

"The auction's over. We won."

"Thank God." He paused, then asked: "Were there any . . . er, personal losses?"

"No," Remo said.

"Good," Smith said, his mind relieved because there would be no international incident.

"Just a minute," Remo said, then called out: "Chiun, what time are you going to be done there?"

Chiun said: "3:30. I have had trouble with this apparatus."

Remo turned back to the phone. "Chiun will be at your headquarters by 4:30. By cab. Have someone meet him to pay the cabbie."

"Give him the money yourself," Smith said. "God knows you draw enough of it."

"Won't work," Remo said. "He won't hand the money through those money slots. Says it makes him feel like a criminal. Just have someone there to pay the cabbie. Chiun will have the lists from our lady friend. They're something to see. Cabinet officers, department directors, senators, congressmen, a presidential assistant. Oh, and a communications specialist. I'll bet that's how we were compromised. I just hope the list's complete."

"How did the thing work?" Smith said.

"Drugs and hypnosis. They were triggered to go off when they heard a certain word. With the lists and the instructions, you should be able to put them back under and bring them back to normal."

Smith thought a moment before answering. "Yes, I suppose so. Although I guess they can never be trusted again in sensitive jobs. We can't just go firing the congressmen, though." He paused. "Maybe they'll accept a suggestion to announce their retirements."

"Any way you want to work it," Remo said. "Chiun'll have the lists. He'll also have the bids that were entered today. They might be good for something."

"You say it was a word that was the trigger?" Smith asked.

"Yes," Remo said. "A line from that song." He had feared this moment.

"What was the song?"

Remo cleared his throat nervously. "Are you listening, Dr. Smith?"

"Yes, dammit, I'm listening."

Remo spoke slowly. "Super-kali-fragil-istic-expi-ali-docious. You will forget that I ever existed. The experiment eight years ago failed, and the man known as Remo Williams died in the chair. He does not exist."

There was a long pause. Back at Folcroft, a beatific smile crossed Smith's face. He began to hum the tune softly into the mouthpiece of the phone. Then he said:

"Forget it. You're in this, Remo Williams, until death do us part. I'll expect Chiun with the lists."

He hung up, chuckling.

Remo's hands were wet as he hung up the telephone back in Manhattan. But he was not done yet.

He watched Chiun putter around until the last problem of the day had been postponed on the last of his television shows. Remo picked up the lists from the floor and, along with the envelopes containing the bids, stuffed them into a large manila envelope he found in the hotel-room closet.

Then he walked downstairs with Chiun and called two cabs. As he helped Chiun into the first cab, he told him: "Remember, Chiun, give these to no one but Smith. I'll contact you at Folcroft soon."

"At my age, am I now to be lectured on caution?" Chiun asked.

Remo ignored him and leaned into the front of the cab. "The trip's to Rye, New York. Folcroft Sanitarium." Remo remembered Smith's habits and pulled a roll of bills from his pocket. He tossed a twenty to the driver. "Here's your tip in advance. Now don't go talking to the old fellow. Don't get him sore. And drive carefully or you'll never hear the end of it."

"Gotcha, mister," the cabbie said, pocketing the twenty and lurching away from the curb in a screech of tires.

Remo got into the second cab. "Kennedy Airport," he said.

On the long rocky ride through afternoon traffic, Remo tried very hard not to think. He tried not to think of how he had breathed easier when he saw that Smith had not been compromised. Remo tried hard not to think on the plane to Washington. He tried not to think about the compromised men who could be transferred, put into jobs where they would not have a real chance ever again to expose America by their weakness. And in the cab from the Washington airport, he tried not to think of the last piece in the puzzle. The possibility that Lithia's list had not been complete; that there was one more man and that man could not be transferred if he had been compromised. He tried not to think of what could happen if that man mentioned CURE's existence, or if that man folded when the chips were down.

He was still trying hard not to think about it when the cab driver interrupted him.

"Here you are, Mac. 1600 Pennsylvania Avenue." The cabbie looked out the window at the large white building behind the metal fence.

"That guy's got a helluva job in there. I hope he knows what he's doing."

"He'd better hope, too," Remo said, giving the driver a twenty and stepping out onto the curb without waiting for change. Washington smelled fresh in the early evening, and the White House looked imposing. Remo noticed the guards at the front gate and smiled.

Smith met Chiun's cab personally when it rolled up to the locked gates of Folcroft. He helped Chiun from the taxi. Chiun clutched the manila envelope of papers to his chest. "How much?" Smith asked the cabbie.

"Nineteen seventy-five," the driver said. Smith extracted a twenty from his wallet, rubbed it between his fingers to make sure two had not stuck together, and passed it through the window. "Keep the change," he said. He turned to Chiun as soon as the cab had lurched away. "Where is Remo?"

"He said he had other business, and he would see you or he wouldn't," Chiun said.

Smith walked inside with Chiun, who left him outside the main building to take his evening stroll. Smith took the manila envelope and went back to his office in the rear of the building, overlooking the sound.

He pursed his lips as he read the names and notes that Remo had taken from Dr. Forrester. It was a cross-section of the American government, so it would be necessary to deal with each one individually. Smith spent several hours studying the names, and working out a complex, detailed program for bringing all the men out of their posthypnotic state. It would be delicate. He would need the assistance of the president.

Smith's hand reached toward the telephone when it rang sharply. He lifted the receiver to his ear.

"Smith."

The familiar voice crackled into the phone sharply. "I thought you told me this afternoon everything was all right again."

"I did."

"Well, they've penetrated. They've gotten past my security. They're right here in the White House."

Smith leaned forward in his chair. "Just a moment, Mr. President. Please tell me precisely what happened."

"I was walking down the hallway outside my bedroom. And then this evil-looking man jumped out from behind a curtain and stepped in my way."

"What did he do, sir?"

"He didn't do anything. He just stood there."

"Did he say anything?" Smith asked.

"Yes, he did. Some kind of nonsense. Super-fragile or something."

"What did you do?" Smith asked.

"I told him, look, fella, you better get out of here or I'll call the Secret Service. And he left."

"Then what did you do?"

"I called the Secret Service, of course. But they couldn't find him. He was gone. Doctor, do you think you should assign that person here until this entire business of selling our government is concluded?"

"It is concluded," Smith said stiffly, "as I advised you this afternoon. And that person has been there."

"You mean . . .?"

"Yes."

"What was he doing?"

"He was guaranteeing our nation's freedom, Mr. President. I will be in Washington tomorrow and I will explain it to you fully."

"I wish somebody would," the president said, then added, "So that was him, eh? He didn't look so tough."

Biography

Warren Murphy and Richard Sapir

Warren Murphy was born in Jersey City, New Jersey. He worked in journalism, editing, and politics. After many of his political colleagues were arrested, Murphy took it as a sign that he needed to find a new career and The Destroyer series was born. Murphy has five children Deirdre, Megan, Brian, Ardath, and Devin, and a few grandchildren. He has been an adjunct professor at Moravian College, Bethlehem, PA, and has also run workshops and lectured at many other schools and universities. His hobbies are golf, mathematics, opera, and investing. He has served on the board of the Mystery Writers of America and has been a member of the Private Eye Writers of America, the International Association of Crime Writers, the American Crime Writers League, and the Screenwriters Guild.

Richard Ben Sapir was a New York native who worked as an editor and in public relations, before creating The Destroyer series with Warren Murphy. Before his untimely death in 1987, Sapir had also penned a number of thriller and historical mainstream novels, best known of which were "The Far Arena", "Quest" and "The Body," the last of which was made recently into a film. The New York Times book review section called him "a brilliant professional."

Printed in the United States
144803LV00002B/26/A